# Letters from Rapunzel

# Letters from Rapunzel

### SARA LEWIS HOLMES

HarperCollins*Publishers*

Library of Congress Cataloging-in-Publication Data
Holmes, Sara.
Letters from Rapunzel / Sara Holmes.— 1st ed.
p.   cm.
Summary: Through a series of letters written to a post office box,
twelve-year-old Cadence describes her father's hospitalization for
depression, her subsequent problems at school, and her hope that the
mysterious recipient will help her find a happy ending.
ISBN-10: 0-06-078073-8 (trade bdg.)
ISBN-13: 978-0-06-078073-9 (trade bdg.)
ISBN-10: 0-06-078074-6 (lib. bdg.)
ISBN-13: 978-0-06-078074-6 (lib. bdg.)
[1. Depression, Mental—Fiction. 2. Fathers and daughters—Fiction.
3. Schools—Fiction. 4. Gifted children—Fiction. 5. Fairy tales—Fiction.
6. Letters—Fiction.] I. Title.
PZ7.H7376Let 2006                                        2006000805
[Fic]—dc22                                                      CIP
                                                                AC

Typography by Larissa Lawrynenko
1 2 3 4 5 6 7 8 9 10

First Edition

*For Mike,*
*who knows my name*

# Part One

*(In Which Rapunzel
Attempts a Rescue)*

2:02 a.m.

Dear Box #5667,

Let me get right to the point. It's the middle of the night, I can't sleep, and YOU are the pea under my mattress.

This letter's about my dad, Aaron Brogan. I found a piece of a letter he was going to mail you, torn up and stuck down the side of his chair. That's how I got your address (part of it, anyway—I couldn't find your name).

I couldn't make sense of most of the letter, since it was only a piece, but the part I could read said:

> . . . *You are the secret to my success as a poet and a human being. Writing these letters every day has helped me keep my heart open, to be willing to live, to keep the darkness . . .*

The rest was torn off. I wish I'd found it sooner. Maybe then I could've written you right away, and asked you how to save him. Because last week he fell victim to the Evil Spell again.

The last time this happened, he had to be away for three days. This time, he's already been gone a week. And now my mom says it could be another month! So if you've been wondering why he hasn't written you, that's why. But please, please, don't give up on him.

My mom says it's an illness, not an Evil Spell, but I know I'm right. Dads don't stop talking just because they're sick. Dads don't forget that their daughters are supposed to get off the bus at 3:05, and they don't sit in the house with the lights out and not answer the doorbell when it rings. Dads, at least my dad, are home every day to meet you and have popcorn and root beer.

I have to get to sleep now, before Mom gets home from work. She's usually not this late, but I guess there was a baby rush. Her record's twelve babies in one night. I think that's why I'm an only child.

Sincerely,
Rapunzel

P.S. That's not my real name. After all, I don't know

YOUR real name yet. And yes, I know Rapunzel didn't have a pea under her mattress. Wrong story. I'll explain tomorrow. Tomorrow I'll have LOTS of time to write.

P.P.S. Tell me about you. How long have you been my dad's friend? Where did he meet you? Are you a poet too?

2:55 p.m.

MONDAY

*(Day One of My Captivity)*

Dear Box #5667,

As I told you last night, I have lots of time to write you today. Without my dad at home after school, my mom signed me up for the Homework Club, which isn't a club at all. It's two tables in the cafeteria. Oh, and one faded black and white sign that reads:

## STUDY HALL! IT'S WHERE YOU WANT TO BE!!!!

I'm sitting with my back to that sign right now, trying to avoid the wrath of the Homework Witch. (They call her the Homework Coach, but when I asked for notebook paper, she hissed and pointed to the propped-up sign at the end of the table that said, "Be prepared. Paper and pencils NOT provided.") That's why this letter's on the back of my math homework from last week.

I hope you don't mind me writing you another letter even though I just wrote you last night and you haven't written me back yet. I know letter writing is supposed to be like Ping-Pong—back and forth, back and forth, back and forth—but you're my only chance at figuring out what to do. Mom says the Evil Spell is bad this time, except she doesn't call it that, of course. That's my name for it. She calls it "C.D."

My mom likes to abbreviate things a lot. She leaves sticky notes on the dishwasher that say, "Plz unld. Thx!" One time, I saw her list for the store and it said,

> 2 pkg. t.p.
> lg. d.w. soap
> apls., prs., grps.
> VGTBLS!!!
> m&c
> lnch. mt.
> rtbr.
> 10 pr. ptyhs.

(That last one's panty hose, in case you're wondering.)

But anyway, I already knew the Evil Spell was worse this time, because yesterday, before my mom went to work, I asked her if I could call my dad, and she said,

"His medication is making him sleep a lot,"

and I said, "I'll call when he's awake,"
and she said, "Be patient, honey,"
and I said, "He's still not talking, is he?"
and then she didn't say anything, and I knew.

She was going to be late for work, but I followed her to the car, and I said,

"Does he have anything to write a letter with? I could send him paper and his blue pens and you could—"

"He can't write you, honey," my mom said. "I'm sorry, but he just has to concentrate on getting better."

I started to tell her it wasn't me he needed to write, it was you, and how you were the secret to his success, but then I realized I'd have to admit to reading a letter that didn't belong to me. And before I could think of any other way to tell her, she was pulling out of the driveway.

But how will he escape from the Evil Spell if no one helps him? I can't do much, at least not while I'm locked up here in Homework Club. But here's my idea. I'll write you in his place, every day if you want me to. And you can write me back, and together we can rescue him.

I think I'll be good at writing lots of letters, because it's just like talking. Everyone says I talk too much, but that's the beauty of letters, isn't it?

I can talk all I want and you can listen to me how you please—all at once, or in little bits, or over and over if you really like what I'm saying. Just don't feel you have to talk back as much as me. I'm a world-class talker so it would be hard to keep up. If I write ten letters to each one of yours, I want you to know up front, THIS IS OK. I'm not the kind of person who keeps score.

Anyway, I guess if I want your help, I should apologize for calling you a pea last night. And I should probably tell you a few things about myself. Let me begin by saying that I never knew I was Rapunzel. At least not until this week. If you had asked me which fairy-tale character I felt most like, I would've said Goldilocks, because of my wild blond hair. I get that from my mom. (She says she gets her hair mowed, not cut.) Definitely not Sleeping Beauty—I only sleep when I have to. Not Cinderella either, because I dance kind of crazy and I would've snapped the glass heel off that slipper WAY before midnight. But Rapunzel? I never thought much about her. She's not much of a heroine—just a victim in a tower. And her name: My dad and I looked it up once in his dictionary—it's a kind of vegetable! That's like being named Turnip Greens.

So what does vegetable girl have to do with me? Well, for starters, we're both stuck. At least she's in a beautiful stone tower in a fairy-tale wood. I, on the other hand, am doing time in a cafeteria that smells like old tomato sauce. Not that they let you eat during Homework Club. I heard the Homework Witch caught a kid chewing gum last week and made him spit it out into his hand and keep it there the whole study period. Even so, I'm secretly sucking on a jawbreaker. If she catches me, she'll probably make me balance it on my head. Still, I go on eating it, silently and stealthily, like Rapunzel's hair grew, right under the nose of her witch. And like I'm going to go on writing you, right under the nose of the Homework Witch, who's paid to glare at anyone whose pencil stops moving between the hours of 2:50 and 5:05.

The reason I thought of Rapunzel at all is because of my science homework assignment:

*Using what we have learned about simple and complex machines, think of ten possible ways that Rapunzel might be rescued from her tower. Answers may be given in words or in annotated drawings. Be prepared to justify your answers to the class.*

A giant lever. That's the first thing I thought of. With a real giant to operate it. He'd stick one end under the stones at the base of the tower, and pry little Miss Rapunzel's tower right out of the ground. Of course, the fall would probably kill her, but hey, the assignment didn't say we had to keep her alive, did it? I wonder if one day, at the end of Homework Club, they'll find me stuck to this chair and have to pry me out with one of those long spatulas they use to serve lasagna. . . .

*Aaargh.* I don't want to learn about simple machines! When is the answer to a problem ever simple? When it's STUPID, that's when. Like my lever and Rapunzel. Simple and stupid. Don't get me wrong. It's not that I think the assignment's a bad one. It's, as far as homework goes, much better than, say:

*List the six simple machines. Give three examples of each type and explain why they are useful to humankind. Any answer that deviates, however slightly, from the textbook, will be soaked in a vat of crimson ink for three days before being tossed into the trash can. (If the student wishes to redo the work correctly, he/she may do so, but it must be resubmitted in triplicate, and only one-tenth of the original grade will be given. NO EXCEPTIONS!)*

No, the assignment's not that bad. The problem is, I'm not interested in doing homework of any kind. What I AM interested in is having my dad come home. Until then, I'm stuck, right here in Homework Club. So tell me: What do YOU know about Evil Spells? And rescues?

Your not-much-of-a-heroine,
Rapunzel

P.S. I don't want you to think I'm a slacker. The girl next to me traded me three sheets of notebook paper for a jawbreaker, so I'm going to do my homework now. I'll stick in a copy of my answers to the Rapunzel question in case you want to see them.

P.P.S. And C.D.—that's clinical depression, not something you want on your grocery list. Ever.

# TEN WAYS TO RESCUE RAPUNZEL

1. Use a giant lever to pry her out. Be prepared for the funeral.
2. Build a large inclined plane against the tower, and grease it well. Attempt to convince Rapunzel she won't get splinters in her butt if she slides down.
3. Rig a system of pulleys to the side of the tower. Attach a large wooden tub to the end of a rope. Use the pulleys to raise the tub up so that Rapunzel can climb in, and then carefully lower her down. (Charge extra if she screams.)
4. Attach a wheel to one end of an axle to make a crank. Use the crank with some rope to hoist a ladder up to Rapunzel's window. Hold the ladder and only jiggle it a little as she climbs down. (Charge extra if she screams.)
5. Tell her to cut off her hair. Take the hair to the market and sell it. Use the proceeds to buy a hydraulic platform (a complex machine made of levers and such) to rescue her. This works well if Rapunzel's a bit on the heavy side.
6. Build a ramp (a form of the inclined plane) around the tower, circling up as you go. Insert a long lever into a crack at the bottom of the

tower and begin to turn the tower with the lever until the lower end of the ramp begins to tunnel into the ground like a giant screw. Turn until the tower is screwed all the way into the ground and Rapunzel can step daintily out.

(Okay, I saw this one in David Macaulay's book *The Way Things Work*, but hey, I'll thank him when I meet him. . . . )

7. Weave a large trampoline out of native grass (try to avoid thorny branches) and convince Rapunzel to jump. (Not sure what kind of a machine a trampoline is. A spring, I think, which might be an inclined plane of a sort.) Anyway, it doesn't matter because Rapunzel wouldn't jump onto an untested trampoline anyway, not if she had any sense of self-preservation at all. Or if she were wearing a miniskirt.
8.
9.
10.

Note: Like I said, I'm NOT a slacker. The reason I listed only seven ways of rescue is because I don't want Mrs. Seisnek—that's my math and science teacher—to get too high an expectation of me this early in the year. After all, it's only the end of September. It's better to start low, and let teachers think they have made "a lot of progress" with you by Thanksgiving. I did carefully number my paper all the way to 10 though, so she could see I'd TRIED, but had been UNABLE to think of more answers. . . .

3:22 p.m.

WEDNESDAY

*(Day Three of My Captivity)*

Dear Box #5667,

I only got half credit for my Rapunzel homework. Mrs. Seisnek did not like the "frivolous" way in which I handled the assignment.

"MORE SCIENCE. FEWER SILLY JOKES," she wrote in her crisp block letters. "AND WHERE ARE YOUR OTHER THREE ANSWERS?"

As if the assignment were serious in the first place! I mean, it's not like she asked us to design a bridge or invent a real, working machine. She asked us to rescue a fairy-tale character, right? I guess it didn't matter that I deliberately didn't put in all ten ideas I had—she wouldn't have liked them anyway. Andrew Marchetti got a 105—he listed fifteen ways to rescue dear, sweet Rapunzel, all of them straight from TechTV. Good for him. I hope Rapunzel likes her princes with precision-parted hair and smug looks on their faces, because that's what she'll get if Andrew rescues her.

My mom thinks I should be friends with Andrew because his mom teaches at the same college as my dad. (My mom's very concerned that I don't have any friends my age. I admit that I usually hang out with my dad or our neighbor, Mrs. Booth, who's sixty-seven. But can I help it if we haven't lived here that long—and that everybody at my new school thinks I'm a geek because I can use the word "fortuitous" in a sentence?) But anyway, my dad teaches Creative Writing and Poetry. Andrew's mom teaches Principles of Market Research. I doubt she even knows much about him, or that he has a substitute teaching his classes right now. At least I hope not. I don't want Andrew to know about the Evil Spell. He could turn into Prince Alarming then, if you know what I mean.

Anyway, who cares? Rapunzel's a stupid story anyway. I mean, look at what happens. Her dad promises her, his firstborn child, to the witch, in order to get what? A bunch of green stuff for his pregnant wife, that's what! What kind of a dad would do that? And then when the witch comes to collect on his promise, does he stop her? Call the law, barricade the door, anything? No, he lets the witch take her! I guess with magic around, he might not have had a chance against the witch, but still, he was stupid to make the promise in the first place. I think people shouldn't promise forever and ever or firstborn children or other things they have no control over. Do you think they do it because they get scared?

But my dad would never do that. He has a plan to deal with Fear. Like, for instance, when I was five, I couldn't fall asleep at night because I was sure the trees behind our house turned into trolls after midnight, and came to my window to try to kidnap me. So, one night, my dad let me hold his heavy flashlight with the scratched-up silver barrel and the orange sliding Hi-Lo-Off switch. Then he gave me a piggyback ride into the woods behind our house. All the way in, he told me a fairy tale starring ME as the heroine. In the story, I defeated a dragon with a twelve-foot blue tail, and got to be ruler of a kingdom with a root beer river that flowed right through my palace. By the time we got home, we had found two tiny frogs, a cloud of dancing lightning bugs, and an army of mosquitoes, but no trolls. And I was even brave enough to turn off the flashlight for a slow count to ten so I could look at the stars from my dad's shoulders.

Now, whenever one of us is scared to try something new, we dare each other to go Into the

Woods. It's how I got my dad to eat Chinese food for the first time. He usually only likes plain food, like bread and cheese. But now he likes egg rolls, too. And especially the fortunes in the cookies. He pulls his eyebrows together and reads them aloud like they're proclamations from an emperor: "You will be RICH . . . if you keep . . . your HONOR!!" And then he presents the slip of paper to me, and I fold it into a tiny triangle, and add it to the Mason jar beside my bed when we get home from the restaurant. Sometimes I wonder if any of them will come true. Maybe not, but I like having almost a hundred possible futures right there in my room.

Into the Woods is how he got me to go to the top of the Statue of Liberty, too, even though I'm afraid of heights. Have you ever been up there? The stairs go round and round and up and up— and you have to climb every one of them to peek out the holes in her crown. I don't remember the view from the top that well because I could only open one eye and look for about two seconds, but I do remember the shape of the inside of her nose on the way up and she had real nostrils. My dad whispered to me, "Good thing she got over that cold. I heard three people got sneezed right outta here last week."

Anyway, where was I? Oh yeah, what bugs me about the Rapunzel story. Besides the whole stupid promise thing, there's the issue of how she got inside the tower in the first place. She's always shown at a window at the top, but how did she get there? She didn't fly. There have to be stairs, like in the Statue of Liberty. And a door. So why doesn't the prince try to get in that way? A good chop with his ax, and he'd be in! Okay, so maybe the door's thick, too thick for him to get through, but I'm telling you, there IS a door.

And the tower has got to be high. High enough that she doesn't just jump out in desperation. Three stories high, at least, which means a lot of STEEP stairs inside that tower. If she went up and down them each day, she'd be in great shape. Thin thighs, healthy heart, glowing skin—everything those infomercials on TV promise you if you'll just buy their exercise video. My mom has a whole stack of those videos. They're still in the plastic wrappers. She has a little sticky note on them, though, that says, "Rtn for rfnd."

Maybe I should design and sell the Rapunzel Workout, where I lock you in a tower with nothing to do but walk the stairs, grow your hair, and wait for the witch to bring you a diet lunch. Of course, most people wouldn't walk those stairs more than once. They'd sit at the top of the tower and stare out the window as if it were a TV set, waiting for the commercial to be over.

Me? If I were locked in there, I'd count every stair step in the place. Measure them by width and height. I'd want to know that tower backward and forward, so that when rescue came, I'd be prepared. I'd call down to the prince: "I don't know what unit of measurement you use (after all, he might be a prince from a foreign land), but I've measured this tower using this table leg, which I've carefully unscrewed and screwed back each time the witch came. The tower stairs have exactly 373 steps, each of which is this wide (I'd point to the mark on the unscrewed table leg) and this high (more pointing)."

Then I'd toss down the table leg and see if the prince had arrived prepared with a tape measure and tools. And I'd make him do the math to figure out how high the tower was on his own.

Yes, of course, I COULD do the math myself, once I knew how my stick marks converted to his measuring units, but hey—if I'm going to trust him to rescue me, to build a ladder contraption or use pulleys or inclined planes or whatever, don't you think I'd want him to be able to do his own math? Otherwise, "Whoops! The ladder's too short—so jump, Rapunzel!" Or "Oops! I thought that platform would hold your weight. Sorry about all the blood."

No, if a prince is going to rescue me, he's going to have to prove he's smart enough first. At least a three-standard deviant, like me.

More later,
      Rapunzel

P.S. Oh yeah, I didn't tell you that I was a deviant yet, did I? It's because of a test I took. . . . Never mind, this letter's too long already. I'll tell you about it in the next one.

5:14 p.m.

WEDNESDAY

*(or as they say in the movies,*

*"Later that same day")*

Dear #5667,

I'm on the bus, so please excuse the bumpy hand-writing. It's hard to write when you have your back up against a bus window and a notebook on your knees. At least the late bus isn't as crowded as the one that leaves right after school, so I can have a seat to myself.

In my last letter, I started to tell you about this test I took last month. It's supposed to tell you what your "cognitive abilities" are, which basically means "brains," but to me it sounds like your head is one big machine with cogs and spokes. My teachers from last year didn't want me to take it, because my grades were bad, but I think this year, my mom made them give it to me anyway. I didn't care one way or the other about knowing how many cogs I have. But it did get me out of class for TWO HOURS! Anyway, turns out, this test says I'm smart. Not a little smart. Like genius-level smart. (Breathe easy, now. I know it's a shock, but I'll wait while you put your gum back in.)

Now normally, they don't tell a kid her score directly. From what I hear, they keep a student's IQ score locked up like it was KFC's secret recipe. But I opened the letter that they sent home with me last week before Mom got home from work. There was a graph that looked like a boa constrictor that had swallowed an elephant. The elephant bulge was where most people's scores are. Me, I was either the elephant's trunk or his tail, depending on which end of the elephant you supposed the boa constrictor swallowed first. Anyway, I'm what they call "three standard deviations above the norm." (Sounds sinister, doesn't it?)

I bet THAT'S why I got a bad grade on my Rapunzel homework. That's why when it was time to change classes, Mrs. Seisnek pinned me to my seat with her laser-blue eyes and gave me a lecture. Mrs. Seisnek LOOKS like she could be somebody's Fairy Godmother, with her perfectly curled, gleaming white hair, rose-petal cheeks, and dusty-pink fingernails, but she couldn't BE one, because she's not interested in what YOU wish for. She has her own ideas about how you can improve yourself. According to her, the wishes I need granted are to start doing my homework, pull up my grades, and stop causing so much trouble. All so she can recommend me for a special gifted and talented program on Fridays. For people supposedly like me.

"You belong there, Ms. Brogan," she said. (She uses last names when she's SURE of her great idea.) "The GT program was made for big thinkers like you."

Right. Like I even WANT to go to a special classroom with a bunch of snobby elephant trunks. (They'd never think of themselves as tails!)

Well, it doesn't matter because I'm not giving that graph to my mom. She has the heart-rate monitor graph from when I was born pasted into my baby book. And my heights and weights from every doctor visit. (I was born early so that was important right at first, but now it's just embarrassing.) If I give her this graph, it'll wind up framed on our living room wall. I know she'll find out eventually, but if I take the sticky note off her calendar on the refrigerator that says, "Call abt tst rslts," I don't think she'll notice for a few weeks.

Besides, me being smart won't make my dad

come home. Me being smart means NOTHING.
Got to go now. My stop is next.

Sincerely yours,
Rapunzel

P.S. I made my mom promise that when she goes
to see my dad tomorrow, she'll help him call me.
I have so much I want to tell him.

11:56 p.m.

THURSDAY *(just before it turns into Friday)*

Dear Box #5667,

I got to say hello to my dad on the phone tonight. That's it. Hello. He said "Hi, honey," back, only he didn't sound like my dad. His voice was flat, like he had been asleep and someone had woken him up too early.

"Hey, Dad, we're learning about Rapunzel in school," I said. "Can you believe that? All those fairy tales you told me are finally paying off!"

Then there was a big silence. I mean, NOTH-ING.

"Dad? Are you there?" NOTHING.

"Dad, it's me. . . ." NOTHING.

It scared me so much that I stopped breathing. I didn't even know it until my mom got on the phone, and I started sucking in big gulps of air.

"Dad loves you. You know that," she said. "I'll be home soon."

But she isn't. She's still over there at the hospital with him.

At least I have his flashlight to keep me company. It works great under the covers if I prop it on a pillow.

Your friend (whether you like it or not),
    Rapunzel

P.S. I wish my dad hadn't torn up that letter. Maybe that's why the Evil Spell's so bad this time.

P.P.S. Or maybe you don't believe in Evil Spells. Maybe you think fairy tales aren't true. Maybe you think I shouldn't call myself Rapunzel. But maybe those people in the fairy tales didn't think they believed in them either. They thought they were ordinary people, with ordinary names and lives, and they didn't know that stories were going to be told about them for hundreds and hundreds of years. Maybe you think you're an ordinary person who writes letters to my dad, but I know you're not. You're more important than that.

You know how I know? Because I looked for the letters you wrote him, and they aren't here. I searched because I wanted to find out your name, and what kinds of things you told him. But there was nothing but drafts of poems on his desk. He must've taken your letters to the hospital with him. You must be like the straw that gets made into gold, or the pumpkin that gets zapped into a coach. Not ordinary at all.

P.P.P.S. That's why I need your help. I can't go Into the Woods by myself.

3:04 p.m.

FRIDAY *(and counting
the minutes)*

Dear #5667,

I counted it up, and at the end of today I'll have
been in this stupid Homework Club for 675 minutes. That's 5 times after school x 135 minutes =
675 minutes!!! I wonder how Rapunzel counted
time in her tower. (When she wasn't marching
her way to thinner thighs on those stairs.) Probably by how much her hair grew. I asked Mrs. Seisnek today how fast hair grows, and she said,
"About a half-inch a month. Why? Are you thinking of cutting that lovely blond hair?" I told her,
"No way. I did the bald thing as a baby, and I'm
never doing that again."

So that's six inches of hair a year. In the pictures, Rapunzel's hair is always about ten feet
long, which would mean she'd have been in the
tower about eighteen years (assuming her hair's
already a foot long when the witch locks her in at
thirteen years). She never gets any older in that
tower, but her hair does! How weird is that? It's

like her hair's alive and she isn't. But then again, I feel dead in Homework Club every day, so I can relate.

Especially at 3:05. That's when I'd be getting off the bus at home. My dad would be in his faded red chair, the one I love because its arms are fat enough to sit on, and he'd have three or four notebooks in his lap, and a bunch of blue pens (that's his favorite color) wedged in the seat cushion next to him, and his huge dictionary propped under his feet, and he'd be in his professor clothes still, except for his feet, which would have no shoes on, and he'd be working on his poems until the moment I thunked my backpack down on the kitchen floor.

Then he'd wave at me, and say, "Start the popcorn. I've got one more line I need to write down, or I'll lose it." If he were still in his writing trance by the time the popcorn was popped, I'd throw kernels onto his notebook until he looked up. Then he'd move over to the counter with me, and we'd eat popcorn, and he'd write more while I thumbed through his dictionary and tried to find a word that would stump him, like "febricity" (which means the state of being feverish, which he knew—he's hard to stump). Sometimes, if my mom wasn't going to be home until late, we'd pop another bag in the microwave and call it dinner. Or we'd order Chinese takeout.

But instead, here I am at 3:08, with no food, and the Wicked Witch of Where You DON'T Want to Be breathing down my neck if I stare off into space too long. And I have almost two more hours of captivity. I guess that leaves me with nothing to do but homework.

So, here's another assignment for you. (I thought you might want to "play along" as they say on TV!) Here's the deal: We saw a program during social studies about the one hundred most influential people of the last millennium. It was pretty interesting, actually, although some of the choices were bogus. I mean, Christopher Columbus was #7. Don't you think that's a bit high for a dude who discovered America by mistake? And you know what I noticed that's even more interesting? A lot of those influential people—they didn't go to regular school! Edison, Lincoln, Einstein, Newton—this show said they found out most of what they needed to know on their own.

I pointed this out to Mr. Stanley (he teaches English and social studies) and he got kind of irritated about it. Which is surprising, because Mr. Stanley's hard to ruffle. He has shaggy eyebrows, thick, dark brown hair that flops when he talks, and he wears sneakers every day. He looks like a bear who woke up after hibernation and found himself changed into a teacher.

"School's important," he said, "and just because some people managed without it doesn't mean that's the best way for most people." His slow voice sped up. "Be glad you live in a country where school's for everybody and free and where kids don't have to work in factories when they turn seven!" (By the time he got to the end of that sentence, his eyebrows were one dark furry line.)

OK, I agree with that, and I'm sure Mr. Stanley could tell me all about lots of places where I definitely wouldn't want to live, but I still want to know WHY so many influential people didn't have, as they always put it, "formal schooling." I'm guessing that if Edison ever had to go to Homework Club, he would've invented the Homework Coach Eliminator instead of the lightbulb.

Anyway, I'm way off track here, because what I started to tell you was: We are supposed to come up with our own essay about who we think was the most influential person of the last millennium. Can't you imagine the lovely essays glorifying Thomas Jefferson, or Einstein, or Pope John Paul? But I'm not interested in that. What I want to know is who the most influential people of

THIS millennium will be. I look around my class and wonder, Is there someone in here who's going to rock the world? Is it that skinny guy with zits on his forehead who never says a word? Or that pale-looking girl who's always sleeping in class? The thing is, you have to think of which persons, which ideas, which discoveries would wreak the most havoc on the world as we know it. Frightening, isn't it?

Got to get to work now,
        Rapunzel (who's enclosing her own ideas about this millennium for your exclusive enjoyment. Send no payment now.)

P.S. Did you notice I dropped the "Box" in front of your number? I guess that means we are on a first-name basis. And I meant what I said last night—I NEED you to write me. SOON.

## RENOWNED PSYCHIC TELLS ALL!!!
## THE MYSTICAL AND MARVELOUS
## MADAME REEPUNZEEL PREDICTS WHO WILL BE
## THE MOST INFLUENTIAL PEOPLE OF
## THIS MILLENNIUM!!!!!

1. The person who discovers alien life and/or communicates with alien life for the first time. Hello, Universe!
2. The person who discovers how to tap into the 90 percent of our brains that we don't use. What in the heck have we got all those brain cells for?
3. The person who invents a way to eat chocolate even when you're in Homework Club and the Witch is staring right at you.
4. The first female U.S. president—don't you think it's about time????
5. The person who discovers the secret of why teachers assign homework on weekends. And makes them stop!
6. The person who discovers how time works, who explains why I get a queasy feeling in the pit of my stomach whenever I try to imagine eternity.
7. The person who discovers how dolphins think,

who understands the intelligence of animals.

8. The person who revolutionizes the way we humans learn. Maybe this person discovers how to link our minds so that we don't all have the same body of knowledge, but can share as needed, like a hive. There's so much stuff to know; we can't go on each holding all of it inside ourselves.

9. The person who discovers how dreaming works—why we have good dreams and horrible ones, why everything seems to make sense while we're in them and no sense at all once we're not.

10. The person who figures out how to undo Evil Spells.

MINUTE #702
*(of Homework Club)*
MONDAY

Dear #5667,

More trouble at school. I guess they really want me to go to that special program for deviants. The counselor, Ms. Trey, left a message about my test results on our answering machine. I don't know her very well, since she's at our school only two days a week. I've seen her twice: the day I enrolled and the day I took the Brain Cogs Test. Both times she was wearing all black, like a raven. And she's teeny-tiny. A bird in high heels.

On the message, she said she wanted to arrange a meeting with my mom to discuss my poor attitude and underachievement. She said that I qualified in every way for the gifted program, except for my grades. Surprise, surprise.

Luckily, I deleted that message before my mom heard it. And I forgot about it until this morning, when Ms. Trey called me out of math class to her office and asked me for a work number for my mom. Her head was cocked to one side, and she was staring at me. Peck, peck, peck—I could hear her starting to poke into my life. I stalled her by saying that my mom worked odd hours, and slept during the day, so it was better to send her a letter. I figured that way I could intercept it, and write my own reply. I can't have it look like my mom's continually ignoring the counselor—they might send someone out to investigate.

To tell you the truth, I did think about giving it a chance, but then I found out something terrible—Andrew qualified for the program too. I don't think I could stand being in there with him. He has been the biggest creep lately, always bugging me, wanting to know what grade I got on my tests and papers, and making a big deal of it if he scored better than me. Besides that, he has started making comments about what I wear, like today he said, "Nice jeans, Sugar Buns." He's completely disgusting.

Anyway, I got Ms. Trey's letter while I was in Mr. Stanley's class this afternoon. It was sealed in a school envelope, with my mother's name inked on the front in thin, scratchy letters.

"Make sure your mother receives this TODAY," said the sticky note on the outside of the envelope. "TODAY" was underlined three times.

So I've got to work fast. Here's what I'm going to do. Tomorrow I'm going to bring in this lovely, perfectly phrased reply from my "mother":

*Dear Ms. Trey,*

*How kind of you to take an interest in my daughter. I was pleased to see her test results—I've always known what a sharp girl she is. Her dad and I are quite proud of her.*

*Unfortunately, we cannot allow her to take part in your gifted program. You see, we believe that all education should be exactly the same for every student. Otherwise, how can grades be assigned fairly? Besides, as I'm sure you're aware, formal schooling wasn't essential for many of our best minds, such as Edison and Einstein.*

*I'm sorry that I haven't been able to speak with you personally, but my job as a labor and delivery nurse has long and unpredictable hours. Written communication is best.*

*Once again, thank you and please ask Mr. Stanley and Mrs. Seisnek to take it easy on my daughter. They can be quite demanding, you know.*

*Sincerely,*

*Sharon Brogan*

I hope that will be the end of it, because I don't like the way Mrs. Seisnek and Mr. Stanley look at me strangely now, as if they expect me to spew out intelligent thoughts every time I open my mouth.

And they don't cut me any slack anymore either! Like that essay I was supposed to turn in today for social studies? Well, I tried to turn in the list I sent you instead. (Except for #10. I didn't think I should mention Evil Spells in social studies.) It was much more interesting than any dumb essay, I thought, but Mr. Stanley caught me before the end of the day, and handed it back to me. Here's what he wrote on it:

> *Although this is clever, it's not the assignment you were given. Please redo if you wish to get credit for your work. I'll give you one more day.*

And then he wrote in cheery purple ink at the bottom,

> *I know you can do it—you're such a smart girl!*

Ugh!!! I wish everyone would forget about that stupid test.

Wasting away in my tower until you reply,
    Rapunzel

P.S. I'm trying to redo my essay for social studies, but the only thing I've come up with so far isn't something I want Mr. Stanley to read.

## THE MOST INFLUENTIAL PERSON
## OF THE MILLENNIUM

Forget about Mother Teresa. George Washington. Thomas Edison. My dad's the most influential person of the last millennium. At least, to me he is.

Did you know he writes me a letter, with a poem in it, every year, for my birthday? Half the time I don't understand the poem—not completely anyway—but it doesn't matter. Understanding isn't the point. It's how those poems make me feel. I read them to myself at night, sitting cross-legged on the bed, catching the words on the paper like they were fantastical beasts in the round, pale moonbeam of his silver flashlight. In the daylight, the words seem to run away when I try to read them, but at night, safely circled by my mighty beam, they slow down and turn toward me, and I whisper them to myself, memorizing their tracks on the page.

That's what I love about my dad—he doesn't give me cute or fancy verses for my birthday. He gives me strange and beautiful and mysterious pools of words, way over my head, but right at eye level with my heart.

Those poems make me feel I'm truly growing older, that it isn't just a cake-and-icing-induced hallucination.

I know it's too early to worry about it yet, but what will I do if October 23rd comes this year and there's no letter or poem underneath my plate at breakfast?

11:30 p.m.

*Still* MONDAY *(at least for another half hour)*

Dear #5667,

I wonder if Rapunzel had as much trouble sleeping as I do. You'd think that being in a tower would be nice and peaceful, but maybe not. Maybe your thoughts get louder and louder when you're alone with them. And I have very loud thoughts tonight. Like these:

I REALLY, REALLY need to talk to you about my dad. My mom helped him call me again tonight and he still sounded strange, like he was reading from a script. He did say more words this time: "How's school?" "Are you helping your mom?" "I love you."

But there was no sparkle in his voice, and my throat started to swell up, and then I couldn't talk at all, and my mom finally had to get on the phone and tell me to hang up. I know it's because of the Evil Spell, but that kind of experience makes me almost not want to talk to him. You've got to help me.

So why aren't you? I really thought there would be a letter from you waiting for me when I got home from Homework Club today. But there was nothing but three bills, a health food catalog, and pizza coupons. I know you're getting my letters because I'm putting them in the mailbox down the street myself. Every day.

So why are you not writing me back or even acknowledging that I exist? Are you mad at my dad? I don't even know if you're a man or a woman. If you're a woman, you had better not be messing around with my dad. My mom loves him, you know. They have been married fifteen years. He always takes her out on their anniversary and they go dancing. My mom loves to jitterbug, and waltz, and swing, but my dad hates it, but he takes her anyway because he LOVES her.

Really, I don't think you're messing around. My dad's way too happy with my mom for that. But how come he writes you and doesn't call you? And if you have a post-office box here, doesn't that mean you live close, and wouldn't you meet him for coffee or lunch sometimes or come by the house? Are you sick? Are you under an Evil Spell too? Or is someone holding you captive? Or maybe you're on vacation and are having your mail held. I need to go down to the post office and ask them about your box number. But I can't because of Homework Club.

I want you to know that this is weird, me writing someone I don't know. I've never done it before. It's definitely Into the Woods for me. The only reason I'm doing it is because I can't do anything else to help my dad. And I thought you might be able to tell me some things about him. Things I need to know.

Like this: Was my dad planning to buy a bridge?

Seriously. I got out my dad's dictionary to see if I could find words to stump him with the next time I get tongue-tied on the phone, and I found a newspaper clipping about a bridge folded up in the back.

### HISTORIC BRIDGE OFFERING

The U.S. Army Corps of Engineers, New England District (NAE), invites written proposals to relocate, rehabilitate, use and maintain the superstructure of the center span of the Breakers Point Railroad Bridge. The bridge is being removed by NAE under authorization by the Water Resources Development Act of 1986. It is one of 25 surviving swing bridges in the area.

The bridge is available for relocation

immediately. Title to the bridge will be tro
ferred subject to the recipient agreein
rehabilitate and maintain the structu.
accordance with the Secretary of the Inte-
rior's "Standards for Rehabilitation." The
recipient will be responsible for any costs
associated with dismantling, hauling and
rehabilitating the bridge. There will be no
charge for title to the bridge.

I went and showed the clipping to my mom, and
asked her if Dad was trying to buy this bridge,
and she got up and left the room. Just like that.
She went into the bathroom and didn't come out
for ten minutes. And then when she did come out,
she gave me a lecture on not wandering around
the neighborhood or going anywhere without her
permission.

"I'm not going anywhere, Mom," I yelled. "How
can I, when I'm stuck in that stupid Homework
Club every single day? Why can't I just come
home, like a normal kid, and call you when I get
off the bus?"

"It's not up for discussion," she said in her I'm
Trying Very, Very Hard to Stay Calm voice. "You
have to have somewhere safe to go after school,
and there isn't anywhere else."

"What about Mrs. Booth? Didn't she used to check in on Grandpa when he lived here? She wouldn't mind staying home for me."

"Mrs. Booth has a brother in a nursing home. And she volunteers nearly every day. It's enough that she looks in on you in the evenings and on weekends. I know you dislike Homework Club . . ."

"HATE it, Mom. Not dislike. HATE. . . . I also DESPISE it . . . DETEST it . . . ABHOR it. . . ." I stopped because I could see Mom was about to quit trying to be Very, Very Calm.

She said, "So you DON'T CARE for Homework Club. I understand that. But I don't have another option right now. Maybe I could ask someone— Andrew's mom, maybe—if you could go to their house, but I haven't had time to—"

"No way," I told her. "I'd rather be found dead in Homework Club than go to Andrew's."

I wish I had the courage to ask her about you. About who you are, and whether I could meet you. After all, you're my dad's friend, and he must trust you. But I'm not sure my Mom does. And she might go into the bathroom again.

So, do you know anything about my dad buying a bridge? I think it might be the one my dad told me about the day we moved into this house, which was his old house growing up, but it's ours now

46

that Grandpa died and left it to us. We were taking Grandpa's stacks of travel magazines and old maps off bookshelves to make room for my dad's poetry books and I asked my dad how come there weren't any kids in this neighborhood and what did he do for friends when he was growing up here.

"Oh, there used to be lots of families that lived on this street," he said. "The Shletskys, the Walters, the Bigmans—and Mrs. Booth next door, she had five kids, all grown up now."

I tried to imagine Mrs. Booth as a young mother. I couldn't, as much as I like her. She's completely covered in brown spots and wrinkled from the hours she spends in her garden. She's a retired real estate agent, but I think of her more like a retired Good Fairy. She's always bringing over snippets of herbs, and old cookbooks that are falling apart at the seams (which my mom reads, and puts sticky notes on recipes like Brandy Braised Roast Beef, and Minted Lamb Shanks with Carrot Curls, and then eats salad for dinner again). Sometimes, Mrs. Booth makes huge pots of very strong onion soup, which we keep for two weeks in our fridge before I pour it down the drain.

My dad went on, "I bet there were ten or eleven of us that ran around like a pack of wild dogs in the summertime. Nobody would worry about us or even expect to see us until dinner, so we had time to ride our bikes anywhere we wanted, even the river."

"How far away was that?" I said.

"About an hour," my dad said. "It's on one of Grandpa's maps, I'm sure. There's a wonderful bridge there that can swing open."

"Like a drawbridge on a castle?" I said.

"No, it's more like a clock. The whole middle section of the bridge sits on a pivot, and when it's closed, that's like six o'clock, straight across the river. Most boats can pass under. But if a tall one comes through, the middle section turns until it's quarter to three. Then there's a passage on either side."

"Can I see it?" I asked.

"Sure, we'll drive up there," he said.

But we haven't yet.

This could be the same one. It sure sounds like it. But why would he want to own a whole bridge? I guess there are some things you could do with it. For one thing, it would be great as part of a playground, especially if you could get the swinging mechanism to work. Or you could put it inside a huge warehouse, and turn the whole place into a river-themed restaurant, and let people eat under it, and on it, and next to it. That would be cool.

Of course, if you had a real river in your back-yard, you could set it up there and use it every day. You could even make it your own personal work of art—you know, graffiti it up with interesting sayings and paintings.

Or maybe my dad was planning to write a poem about the bridge being sold. It's the kind of thing that used to make him get an odd look on his face, like he was way off in another world. One time he said poetry happened whenever he felt "the weight of reality's shadow." I didn't get that exactly, but then he said it was like the world tilted, or shifted a little, so that he could see its hidden side.

That I get. Happens to me late at night, but who's around then to tell anything to? Except you, and I don't mean to make you mad, but you aren't turning out to be what I expected.

Good thing Rapunzel doesn't change into any-thing at midnight because I'd be a pumpkin by now.

Got to go,
Rapunzel

P.S. Am I doing okay with these letters? I'm sure my dad wrote to you about lots more interesting stuff, but this is the best I can do. I tried to liven this one up with a little dialogue. Mr. Stanley says dialogue's important. But the thing about it is, you need two people.

Dear #5667,

Ms. Trey found out that letter from my mother was a fake. I guess I made it a little over the top to be believable. I mean, my mom isn't going to talk about Edison and Einstein to a school counselor! And why did I mention Mrs. Seisnek and Mr. Stanley? That was a BIG mistake—Ms. Trey showed them the letter, and they recognized my handwriting. I guess I wrote what I wanted to write, and not what my mother would've really said. And I forgot that letters are different from a phone conversation. Your words are right there, in black and white, and can be studied, and thought about, and shared. Which is a good thing, if your words are wonderful, like my dad's poems, or maybe like his letters to you, but not when you wish you could take them back.

So anyway, yesterday, when Ms. Trey blew my cover, she called me to her office and gave me a lecture on how forgery is a serious offense and she expected more from me. I stared at her shiny black shoes the whole time, and tried to guess how high the twigs that held them up were, and if they'd snap off if someone bigger than a bird, like me, tried them on. At least I got off without a suspension because I managed to look scared and sorry (although I wasn't) and because I told Ms. Trey I'd try harder to live up to my potential. And (she drives a hard bargain) I had to cough up my mom's work number.

Then, just like I thought, once my mom found out about my test scores, I was trapped.

"Why do you think I had you take that test?" she said. "I already knew you were smart. It's just that YOU don't know it. Or act like it. You should be learning more in school than forgery and deception."

She made me write a formal note of apology to Ms. Trey (that's why I didn't have time to write you in Homework Club yesterday) and even worse, she says I have to try attending the gifted program, at least once. (Gifted. What a stupid thing to call it. It makes me feel like I'm a big present, wrapped up in shiny paper with a fluffy bow for people to pat and admire.) I guess Ms. Trey and my mom think that once I see how wonderful it is, I'll be more motivated and cooperative. As far as I'm concerned, school is school. How great can it be?

My trial gifted day will be next Friday. (It was going to be this Friday, but it's a Teacher Workday and there's no school! Yeah!!!) My mom's even letting me stay home by myself because Mrs. Booth isn't volunteering that day and agreed to check in on me. My mom tried to suggest Andrew's house again, but I told her I'd rather keep Mrs. Booth company and help her water her plants. Mrs. Booth has a jungle in her house. She even has orchids and Venus flytraps.

Still growing my hair,
    Rapunzel

P.S. Check out this story I started writing during math class. I can't make up new tales like my dad can, but I'm pretty good at twisting old ones around. And it's the only thing keeping me sane while we review how to set up word problems again. Except Mrs. Seisnek says we should really think of them as word OPPORTUNITIES. Ha!

# MUCH ADO ABOUT A MATTRESS

### Part One
#### (OF A TRULY TWISTED TALE)

### BY R. A. PUNZEL

I lay in the dark, perched high on a tower of twenty-two fluffy mattresses, unable to sleep a wink for the fourth night in a row. What cruel test had been slipped under my bedding this time? Another vicious pea? A cucumber seed? A hummingbird claw? Or perhaps I was being tortured by cat dander. Ugh!

One thing was certain: Someone still doubted I was a real princess. The wedding was next week. If I didn't find out who the doubter was soon, I was going to walk down the aisle as bruised as a tomato bounced from a farmer's wagon.

The next morning, I detained the serving girl, Josina.

"There was primrose pollen under my mattress last night," I said. "How did it get there?"

"Wouldn't know, miss," she said. Her eyes

54

were puffy, as if she had rubbed onions in them. "I just bring the breakfast."

She plopped down a tray heaped with steamed broccoli. Yesterday, it was three crocks of asparagus.

"Is there someone here who doesn't like me, Josina?" I asked.

Josina yanked at her greasy hair. "The Royal Pursekeeper does keep yelling, 'No dowry, no wedding!'" She tossed a fork beside the broccoli and slouched out of the room.

It was true that I'd been left at the steps of the Perfect Princess Academy without a dowry. Was the Royal Pursekeeper trying to scare me off and save a bundle by canceling the wedding? I went to confront him.

"Someone's been sabotaging my bed," I said. "Peas, grains of sea salt, grasshopper legs, and now primrose pollen!"

"Primrose pollen," he huffed. "That's for the wedding cake. Do you know how much that stuff costs?" He whipped out a long scroll and proceeded to tell me. "And then there are the four golden tassels for the ring bearer's cushion," he went on. "Do you know how much they cost?"

Obviously the Royal Pursekeeper was not

my culprit. He would've used something cheap, like more peas.

"Never mind about tassels and cushions," I said. "Tell me where the primrose pollen is kept."

"In the kitchen with the wedding cake decorations, I presume," said the Royal Pursekeeper. "That is, if there's any pollen left. I suppose I shall be forced to order more." He rustled his scroll at me as I hurried away toward the kitchen.

When I got there, I found Cook humming to herself as she stirred a steaming cauldron of watercress stew.

"The primrose pollen for the wedding cake," I said. "Is any of it missing?"

"Why would any of it be missing?" said Cook. She reached over and buttoned the top two buttons of my dress. "Where's your sweater, dear? You'll catch cold before the wedding."

"It's hot enough to cook waffles on the roof," I said, unbuttoning my top button so I could breathe again. "My real problem is getting rid of these bruises!" I showed her my latest battle scar and told her about my mattress troubles.

"Is there someone who doesn't want me to marry the prince?" I asked.

"Well, there's Josina," said Cook. "She's got a crush on the prince, you know. I told her not every serving girl is as lucky as Cinder Ella, but she's heartbroken, poor thing."

Josina, in love with the prince? This put a whole new spin on things. Maybe she was trying to break up my wedding out of jealousy. But if I accused her outright, she might simply deny everything. I decided to wait until that night and catch her in the act. . . .

TO BE CONTINUED!!!!

Dear #5667,

You know, I thought this would work, writing you, but it isn't so great when you don't write back. I don't know what I hoped for, but at least a sense that my words weren't flying off into outer space.

So I'm taking this letter straight to the post office myself. Tomorrow. Maybe you closed your post-office box. Maybe you're dead. Maybe you just don't want to carry on a friendship with me. But I'm going to find out.

Yours most determinately,
Rapunzel

P.S. Did you know they make deodorant with names like Ambition and Optimism? That's what I need to track you down and break the Evil Spell—a little roll-on ambition. . . .

3:05 p.m.

FRIDAY

Dear #5667,

I don't know if I should keep writing to you or
not. After I helped Mrs. Booth with her plants, I
told her I was going to ride to the library, which
I did, but then afterward, before I headed home,
I went farther. I rode down to the main post
office and found your box. It was a little high
up for me, being on the top row, but I could
see through the tiny glass window if I stood on
my toes, and even from that angle, I could tell
it was stuffed. Why aren't you getting your
mail?

I waited in a long line at the counter to ask
about you, but they wouldn't tell me anything,
not even your name. I said I had been writing to
you, and that you hadn't picked up your mail,
and what could I do, and the postal clerk
shrugged and said, "That's why people get
boxes—so they don't have to get their mail held
when they go out of town. We only get involved if
the mail overflows the box."

"But what if the person who owns the box is dead?" I asked. "Or kidnapped?"

That snotty postal clerk laughed.

"Who are you, Nancy Drew?" she said.

"Who are YOU?" I wanted to say, "Dumbo, the elephant???"

But I didn't. I studied the Wanted posters for a while, checked out the new stamps, and looked up my name in the ZIP code book to see if there was a town named after me. There wasn't, at least not in this state. I went back to the counter to mail you the letter I'd brought, and the postal clerk wouldn't put it in your box without a stamp! Can you believe that? It costs the same for them to walk the letter to your box as it would to mail it from across the country. Well, I didn't have any stamps with me, or any money either, so I tore up the letter and put it in the trash.

Maybe that's why my dad tore up his letter too. Maybe you stopped writing him, and he got so upset at you that he quit. Or maybe he stopped writing you first, and then you got mad at him. I don't know. I don't know anything!

Alone in my tower,
    Rapunzel

P.S. I don't even know if I'm going to mail this letter. It's going to wind up in that little box with the rest of them.

P.P.S. I looked up stuff about the Evil Spell at the library. They have a lot of books, and magazine articles, mostly about new medications. But Evil Spells aren't something you can break with a book. If they were, then my dad would've done it already. He owns about a thousand books.

The scariest thing I found out is that the Evil Spell runs in families. Like if somebody close to you has it, then your chances of being zapped by it are more than the average Joe-on-the-Street. That means me.

And it turns out that being smart doesn't help you either. Everyone thinks that smart people are happy, but it's not true. What's so happy about being able to see what's wrong all the time, and not having the power to fix it? What's so happy about feeling weird and different every day of your life? What's so happy about having gorgeous, superlative, wonderful hair (or a BRAIN) when you're kept in a tower?

1:33 a.m.

*(past Sunday night and into
Monday morning)*

Dear 5667,

I think the Evil Spell's getting me too. My mom
didn't have to work tonight, so we went out to the
China Happy Palace, and I could hardly eat anything. Especially after I said I was wondering if
Dad was going to be able to give me my poem on
my birthday this year, and she said, "He can
hardly talk on the phone, honey. I don't think you
should expect too much, at least not for another
couple more weeks. . . ." And then I guess she saw
the look on my face, or maybe she remembered
that my birthday was in LESS THAN two weeks,
because she started going on and on about how
Dad was doing the best he could to get well, and
how unpredictable C.D. was.

"C.D., Mom?" I surprised myself because I fired
that out of my mouth loud enough that the restaurant got quiet for a second. I lowered my voice
and said, "A CD is what you listen to music on."

"Well, okay, then," she said slowly. She took a

tiny sip of egg drop soup. "Clinical depression."

"The Evil Spell," I said back, just as slowly.

"I don't know where you get that," she said. "It's an illness. Like cancer. Well, not cancer, because that's cells growing out of control, and C.D. is more like your whole self shutting down. But it's not a spell."

"It is," I said. "Ask Dad."

"I can't," she said. "He's not talking much to me either."

She started slurping her egg drop soup, louder than I'd ever heard her slurp before.

After that, the egg rolls tasted like rolled-up dead leaves, even after I drowned them with plum sauce, and we wound up taking most of my garlic chicken home in a take-out box. I told my mom I wasn't too hungry because I'd eaten popcorn all afternoon, but really it was because I couldn't stop thinking about my letters squeezed up together in that little box.

And me, squeezed up in Homework Club tomorrow.

And my dad, the way he looked the day before he went into the hospital, when I had to get the extra key from Mrs. Booth when he didn't answer the door and I found him squeezed up in one corner of his red chair, with no lights on, crying.

I called my mom at work, and she came home and put him in the bed, and the next day, even though she said he wasn't going to the hospital right away, when I came home from school, he wasn't there at all. There was just a note that Mrs. Booth had stuck to our front door telling me to come to her house instead.

If I'd found your torn-up letter that day, I could've done something differently. But I didn't find it for a week, and I guess that was too late. I'm sorry. I'm sorry if you're mad, or sad, or upset.

But that's the way I feel too,

Rapunzel

P.S. Even my fortune cookie message was awful: "Great things will come to those who wait." I'm tired of waiting!!! I have to have a new plan to beat this Evil Spell. I just don't know what it is. But I'm not going to stay squeezed up in Homework Club. And I'm not going to let the Evil Spell get both my dad AND me. Or you. So I'm mailing this letter, even though before too long, my letters may make your little glass window break. Then you'll have to come and get them.

P.P.S. And to make this letter extra fat, I'm including part two of my twisted tale. So there!!!!

## MUCH ADO ABOUT A MATTRESS

### PART TWO
### (IN WHICH THE PLOT AND THE STEW THICKEN!!!)

### BY R. A. PUNZEL

That evening, I watched from inside my wardrobe as Josina brought my dinner. I could see through the crack that it was fried grasshopper crepes and a huge bowl of broccoli. Again.

After Josina dropped the tray on the table, she looked over her shoulder and crept toward my bed. One skinny hand slipped under the bottom mattress. What was she planting this time? I stepped from the wardrobe and grabbed her wrist.

"I know you're jealous of me and the prince," I said. "What were you going to torture me with tonight?" I turned over her hand to see the evidence, but there was nothing there. I searched under my mattresses. Nothing there either. "What were you doing to my bed?" I demanded.

"Oh, miss," said Josina. "I was only looking for leftover primrose pollen. Now that I can't marry the prince, I was going to sell it and use the money to run away."

I didn't believe her. "Then why didn't you pinch some pollen from the kitchen?" I asked. "Why bother my mattresses?"

"Oh, Cook doesn't let me near that expensive stuff," said Josina. "It's locked in the pantry."

The pantry! Of course. Everything that had been slipped under my mattresses had been edible—the pea, the sea salt, the grasshopper legs from the crepes, and the pollen for the wedding cake. But who had the key to the pantry? Cook, for sure. But why would she sabotage my bed? Someone else must have a key. I ran to the kitchen to find out.

Cook was folding up her apron for the night. She looked startled to see me.

"What, still hungry?" she asked. "Didn't you finish your broccoli?"

"Um, no," I said. "But I'd like dessert. From the pantry."

Cook narrowed her eyes. "If you'd eaten your broccoli you wouldn't be hungry now. Besides, I've locked the pantry for the night." She began to shoo me out of the kitchen with her apron.

"But what if the Royal Pursekeeper wants to take inventory of the pantry tonight?" I said. "He's very concerned about missing primrose pollen."

"Then he'll have to do it tomorrow," said Cook, pushing me toward the door. "I'm not staying late for him."

"Of course, he probably has his own key," I said, as innocently as I could.

"Fiddlesticks," said Cook. "That silly man doesn't have a key to my pantry. He'd be counting the salt grains every day if he did. I'm the only one with a key to this . . ." She stopped.

"So it was YOU," I said. "You put that horrible stuff under my mattresses."

TO BE CONTINUED!!!!

3:07 p.m.

MONDAY

Dear #5667,

I keep making up my mind never to write you again, since you never write me, but there isn't anything better to do here in Homework Club. And I somehow have gotten in this bad habit of composing letters to you in my head while I'm on the bus, or during a boring patch at school when I have to look like I am paying attention but I'm not. And then I have to actually write them down or they drive me crazy (even if it's to send them to a strange person who never gets her/his mail and/or acknowledges the daughters of close friends).

Also, I keep thinking that me writing you will bring my dad home sooner. I know that's stupid, like not stepping on cracks in the sidewalk or always wearing the same T-shirt when you take a test, or any of those other superstitions that don't make any sense. But you do them anyway because if you DIDN'T and something bad happened, well, you'd be kicking yourself forever.

I even took home that stupid fortune from last night and put it in my jar. Even though I wanted to tear it into little pieces. My dad never lets me tear up the ones I don't like. Although sometimes he does make one up. Like one time, after he broke open his cookie, he got a concerned look on his face, and read the fortune slowly:

"Help. Please help. I'm being held prisoner in . . ."

"Where, Dad? Where?" I tried to grab the message out of his hands.

". . . in a . . . in a . . . FORTUNE COOKIE FAC-TORY," he said in a fake whisper.

My mom rolled her eyes and said, "Aaron, that's the oldest joke alive." But she was smiling.

I don't know what her fortune was last night. She didn't even break open her cookie.

The most un-fortune-ate,
    Rapunzel

P.S. I think I like stories better than fortunes. You can always rewrite stories if you don't like them. Here's the new ending for my "Princess and the Pea" story.

# MUCH ADO ABOUT A MATTRESS

## PART THREE
### (WHICH IS MORE OF A BEGINNING THAN AN ENDING)

BY R. A. PUNZEL

Cook blinked twice, then said, "Yes, dear, I put those things in your bed." She crooked one finger under my chin. "But I wouldn't have had to if that Perfect Princess Academy I paid for had done its job and taught you some manners."

"You?" I struggled to take a breath. "Why did you pay for my schooling?"

Cook brushed her hands firmly against her skirt and smiled sweetly. "I'm your mother, darling."

I staggered back against the chopping block. "My mother? A cook?"

"Oh, yes. Well, I admit I was only an Assistant Egg Cracker when I married your father, but he was a full prince. It was going to be 'happily ever after' for us, but on your first birthday, a dragon ate him. Burned the kingdom down. I had to send you away for

70

proper rearing, or no one would believe you were a real princess."

I thought of the plates of vegetables, the constant buttoning of my dress, the needless advice. She was definitely my mother.

"But why?" I said. "Why did you keep slipping those things under my mattresses?"

"As long as you kept complaining about your bed, there was going to be something nasty in it. A real princess should never mention a bumpy mattress, no matter how black-and-blue it makes her."

I sank down to the floor.

My mother went on talking. "Remember, when you walk down the aisle, keep your head up. Take tiny steps."

I covered my eyes. I had to be the only princess who ever looked under her mattress and found a mother.

"Teeny-tiny steps. No running, do you hear?"

Keep my head up? No running? That was worse than sleeping on a lumpy mattress.

"Wait a minute," I said to my mother. "Who makes up these rules for princesses anyway? First I was supposed to notice the pea in order to win the prince, but then I

71

wasn't supposed to notice the rest of the icky stuff in order to be polite!"

My mother patted my hand. "Well, dear, I'm sure you'll figure it out, once you're married to the prince. I can't say that I did, when I was married to my prince, but then I was always better at cooking than being royalty."

I thought about this for a minute. A long minute.

Finally, I said, quite firmly and loudly, "And I've always been better at asking questions than at being a princess."

And so it was that I decided not to marry the prince after all. Not to sleep on any more piles of mattresses. Not to take teeny-tiny steps. Instead, I opened my own detective agency, and lived happily ever after, asking lots and lots of questions.

THE END

Dear #5667,

I think I have a new plan! Or a tiny little idea for half of a plan. It depends on whether you can lend me three-quarters of a million dollars by next month. (I can hear you laughing, all the way from Tahiti, or the South Pole, or wherever you've been on vacation, not writing me. But I don't care, because how do I know if you're rich unless I ask? Or maybe you have a rich neighbor. Or a celebrity cat who made millions doing commercials.)

Here's the deal: Remember that bridge from the newspaper? It turns out it IS the one my dad used to play near when he was a kid. The reason I know is that he wrote a book of poems about it. Not one that's published yet. But one he's trying to get published. There was a package for him in the mail yesterday, from Landis Press, so I worked the flap open, and I found out he had sent his manuscript there but they sent it back. I read the letter from the editor, and it said, "Although you have some fine poems in here, we don't feel this collection holds together as a unified work. Furthermore, although the regional interest is strong, we don't feel overall sales will be high enough to justify its publication. Good luck placing it elsewhere." Well, that sure sounds polite, but I know it's a brush-off. Big-time. Like the time my fifth-grade chorus teacher told me that I "pronounced the words to the song well" when what she really meant was that my singing STUNK.

I want to tell my dad that I like his poems, even if the editor didn't. They're about various parts of the bridge, and the bridge in different seasons and weather, and some of them are about him as a kid. The one I like best is about him being dared to kiss this girl for the whole time that a boat was going through the swing lock. And how he closes his eyes and imagines his future with her, but she keeps her eyes open and is looking out over his shoulder at the far shore.

I wonder if he actually did this, and I wonder who the girl was. I don't think it was my mom, because they didn't meet until he was in college. She dropped her backpack on his foot while they were both waiting to catch the bus, and then she had to go with him to the student health clinic because his toe was broken. My mom says they found out each other's name and laughed about how they rhymed (Aaron and Sharon). Then, because it was flu season and the clinic was crowded, they had an hour to talk while they waited. An hour surrounded by sick people doesn't sound romantic to me, but my dad says he thought about faking a seizure so she'd stay and talk to him more. He still has the note she left with him that day: "Sorry abt. yr. toe. Plz call me!"

Anyway, after I read his poems, I decided it was time to go Into the Woods and call about the bridge. I don't think the woman who answered the phone could tell how old I was, because I'm pretty good at faking voices, so I acted like I call government agencies every day and straight out asked her how much money they thought it would take to move, fix up, and maintain the bridge. You know what she said?

You guessed it: three-quarters of a million dollars!!!!

Who's got that kind of money to spend on a bridge? (I'm hoping you do.)

Then I asked, "What happens if nobody buys it?" The lady on the other end hesitated, and then she said, "I guess they'll have to destroy it." Can

you believe that? How can they blow up something that my dad thought was so beautiful that
he wrote a whole book of poems about it? And
there isn't much time left either. That lady said
the deadline was next month. If no one steps forward by then, BOOM! No more bridge.

Why don't the people who know what to DO
with three-quarters of a million dollars ever have
it? Or why don't their friends who have it lend it
to them? (HINT, HINT)

Maybe you don't think this is much of a plan.
Maybe you don't see how saving this bridge could
do anything to break the Evil Spell. To be honest,
I'm not sure myself. I just know that I'd like to
give my dad a gift of good news. A reason to come
home.

At least I got them to give me directions to the
bridge, so that if my mom and I are up that way,
I could go and look at it. Not that we ever go anywhere. . . .

Wishing I knew how to spin straw into gold,
     Rapunzel

P.S. Just in case you don't come through with the
money, I do have some other ideas to save the
bridge.

## TEN WAYS TO SAVE THE BRIDGE

1. Ask three-quarter million people for one dollar apiece.

2. Get a picture of the bridge on the national news. A millionaire will see it and want it for his living room.

3. Sell the international movie rights to my life story. (That's worth, what? Five cents?) Or maybe I could live up there and have them broadcast my daily life on TV?

4. Turn it into a gigantic work of art by letting artists and writers decorate it with their work for a fee. Except most artists and writers don't have a lot of money to begin with.

5. Adopt-a-Bridge. Sell little certificates that said buyers were part owners of the bridge, with a little picture of how their piece fit in with the whole rest of the bridge.

6. Tie myself to the railing and refuse to come down until they promise not to blow it up. (Yeah, right.)

7. See if a big company would sponsor the bridge. No, they'd probably want to paint a gigantic ad on the side of it:
DRINK BIG BUBBLE,
THE ONLY SOFT DRINK THAT'S
GUARANTEED TO MAKE YOU BURP

AFTER ONE SIP!

8. Sell T-shirts that say, "Why did the bridge cross the river?" on the front and "Because it was tired of having to go around" on the back.

9. Find a museum that wants it. Is there a Museum of Bridges?

10. Open a lemonade stand? Except I'd have to charge fifty dollars a cup to make enough money fast enough. . . .

Dear #5667,

This is me, writing you from math class. You'd think Mrs. Seisnek would teach us something practical, like how to raise three-quarters of a million dollars, but she keeps giving us math opportunities like this:

Goldilocks grew up and had three daughters. Baby Bear grew up and had three sons. If each of Goldy's daughters had three more daughters, and each of Baby Bear's sons had three more sons, how many bowls of porridge would there have to be at their fifty-year reunion party?

Well, not really, that's one of my math opportunities. Hers always have to do with crates of fruit and the square footage of warehouses. Anyway, I

1:30 p.m.

Sorry about that. Mrs. Seisnek decided to get nosy, and I had to stuff your letter into my binder. Now

I'm in English class, which should be safer. Except that I think Mr. Stanley thinks I'm weird.

We've been doing this thing in class called freewriting, where he has us write without stopping for five minutes, not worrying about grammar or spelling or even staying on the topic. It's supposed to get you loosened up to write the "real" stuff, like the essays he assigns. Actually, it's kind of fun. The only problem is, I don't want to move on to the "real" stuff. It's, like, you do the freewriting, and it gets you pumped up about a particular topic, and then you have to totally switch gears and write on some stupid thing like "My Favorite Character in a Book" or "Why I'm Proud to Be a Citizen." Well, today we had to write about a small thing that no one notices but that's interesting when observed and described in detail. And then we could read our freewriting out loud, like a speech, if we wanted to.

Now, I know what he had in mind. He wanted us to write about a flower, or an industrious ant, or the veins on a leaf. But I didn't want to write about those things. So this is what I wrote about:

*Good afternoon, fellow classmates. Today I speak to you about snot. Yes, the green, sticky kind that won't come out of your nose when you blow it. That gets under your nails. Not the clear, polite, runny trickle that drips from an allergy or a simple cold. No, here we examine the green gunk that hardens into those satisfying globs that you can pick from your nose and wipe on your jeans or drop over the side of the couch. This hard kind is also polite in its own way because it doesn't run out uninvited. The worst, rudest kind of snot is the bubbles that erupt from your nostrils when you sneeze violently without a single tissue in sight. They can't be politely sniffed away or delicately rubbed with the side of a finger. They demand full-fledged snot-catching action.*

*Then there are the rhymes for snot: not (as in "not me, not my snot"), hot snot, pot of snot, a lot of snot, cot of snot, bought some snot, ought to snot, sought snot, caught snot, robot snot. . . .*

The class was loving it! The boys were laughing (in a good way) and one girl was tapping her hand on the desk in time to my beat. For the first time, I thought I might have gotten the school thing right, and then Mr. Stanley cut me off.

"Thank you so much. What an interesting choice." He grabbed a tissue from his desk and blew his nose. "I believe we understand your feelings about nasal secretions. Next, please!"

Why do teachers encourage you to be creative when they don't mean it?

Sincerely,
    Rapunzel

P.S. I'm going to do some REAL freewriting now. . . .

# FAIRY-TALE FORTUNES

## (GUESS WHICH ONE IS YOURS)

1. Everything you touch will turn to gold.
   Except if it's already gold. Then you get a
   coupon for a free burger.
2. You will huff and puff soon—so get to the
   gym and get in shape!
3. Someday your prince will come. As soon as
   he stops and asks for directions.
4. No one should admire a wolf's teeth except
   his dentist.
5. The third time something ALWAYS happens.
6. You will get turned into a frog, but don't
   worry—your clothes will shrink to fit.
7. If you're locked in a tower, hope that a
   teacher makes a homework assignment out
   of you.
8. Never tell anyone your true name. Or make a
   mysterious old woman mad. Or write about
   snot.
9. You will be asked to write fortunes for a fortune cookie factory. Say no.
10. You will be asked to donate three-quarters of
    a million dollars to a worthy cause. Say yes.

11:58 p.m.

WEDNESDAY

Dear #5667,

I think I found some of my dad's writing. Or maybe it was part of another letter he was going to send you. But I wish I hadn't opened the drawer to his desk. I was only going to look for more stamps for these letters, because I'd run through the roll we keep in the kitchen drawer, but then I saw this paper with his handwriting, so I read it. And now I can't sleep. Here's what he said:

*You must be willing to have your heart broken in order to live. There's no other choice, scramble as we may to look for it, to find a way out of our dilemma. It is hope, crack your heart open and breathe, or close it up and die. And the pain is never less, the fear never less, only we can hope that our weakness and confusion grow less so that we will be able to crack our hearts open, day after day, to love and to hope, the bitterest of emotions.*

*I resent its hold on me. I resent its power. I*
*resent that it forces me to choose it, though*
*my heart would rather not some days. Some*
*days, I'd rather not know about perfection,*
*would rather not be confronted by beauty,*
*would rather not be embraced by hope . . .*

This is the Evil Spell, isn't it? I guess it was already starting to happen to him, except he couldn't see it. Maybe I can sleep if I leave my flashlight on.

Wishing I had a Fairy Godmother,
  Rapunzel

P.S. Why didn't you help him if you knew what was coming? Why won't you help me?

2:23 a.m.

P.P.S. I just woke up from a dream, and my dad was in it. He was living right by the bridge, like a homeless person in a cardboard box, except it was a huge post office box, with a glass door. People kept coming by and putting these tiny letters through a hole in the front, and my dad was collecting them, and smiling and waving. Then, all of a sudden, I saw that there was water leaking into the box, except my dad didn't notice it—he was too busy catching the letters as they came through the slot. I was up on the bridge, and I tried to yell down to him about the water, but he couldn't hear me, and then the bridge started to swing open, and I was still on it, and I was falling, falling, and screaming at the top of my lungs.

My mom came into my room because I was yelling so loudly.

"What's wrong, honey?" she kept saying. "What's wrong? Are you sick?"

I couldn't tell her about the dream. All I could do was hold on to my flashlight, which had burned out . . . click, click, click, nothing—and try not to cry.

Finally, my mom gave up on trying to get me to talk, and said she would put batteries for my flashlight on her grocery list.

3:50 p.m.

THURSDAY

Dear #5667,

I'm too tired to write you today. But I have to. I have to tell you about the strange thing that happened to me in English class. We had a substitute today, and she obviously had no idea that we were supposed to be doing freewriting and not-so-free reading of it aloud. She said she loved Shakespeare, which was pretty cool because she brought a video of scenes from his plays, and then we got to act out lines, which was funny because none of the boys wanted to do it unless it involved a beheading. Anyway, we read a little bit from *Richard II*, about the hunchback king, and there was a part I loved. It went like this:

*"You may my glories and my state depose,*
*But not my griefs; still am I king of those."*

It gave me chills, thinking of the king with nothing left but his griefs, clutching them to himself in a dark room—like my dad . . . .

Then something weird happened. I wrote a poem about it. I didn't mean to, but all of a sudden, it was like there was another SOMETHING in the room, like a ghost. You know how you feel like there's breath on your neck? I didn't know how long it would last, so I grabbed a pen and I wrote down everything I could about that moment.

What I wrote didn't make sense at first, but then I remembered what my dad told me once about his work—that he tried to make his poems like spells (good ones, not evil) so that when someone heard one, the listener would be haunted by the spirit of the poem, as he was when he wrote it. So I went back and tried to make the pieces I'd written fit into a pattern, like I was trying to make a picture of that ghost out of words.

Here's the poem:

### KING OF GRIEFS

*He's the King*
*in riot gear,*
*a mob surrounds his throne—*
*You're mine—and you—*
*and you—you're mine—he tells his fears,*
*but still they moan,*

*knowing he is armed*
*with only poetry*
*and tears—*

It's not perfect, but I hope you like it,
 Rapunzel

P.S. Is this what you've been waiting for? A poem from me? Is THAT how I get you to write me back?

P.P.S. My trial day at the Deviant Program is tomorrow. What if everyone thinks I shouldn't be there? I've never been one of those kids who gets good grades. What if they find out that test was a big mistake?

3:06 p.m.

FRIDAY

Dear #5667,

I had a stupendously bad day, and if I don't put it someplace, I won't be able to get through the rest of the day.

Let's see if I can break it down for you.

THE CIRCUMSTANCES: I had a copy of my poem stuck in my binder, so I could work on it more in Homework Club today.

THE FURTHER CIRCUMSTANCES: My poem FELL OUT of my binder just as I sat down at the back of the GT classroom for my trial day—and Andrew grabbed it before I could stop him.

THE MOMENT OF TRUE DISASTER: He read my poem to the entire class. In a freaky, high-pitched voice, with little gasps and sighs at the end of each line. And then when he saw that I'd signed it "Rapunzel," he fell on his knees and starting moaning, "Oh, Rapunzel, Rapunzel, let down your hair! I'm the King of Grief— Ooooh! Oooh!"

THE CRIME: I hit him. Right in the nose with my English book.

THE PUNISHMENT: A.D.I.S.D. (All-Day In-School Detention) on Monday. Plus, I had to leave the GT classroom immediately. That's probably a record for a new student. And I know they're going to call my mom at work and tell her why.

That about sums it up,
    Rapunzel

P.S. See how much writing you has made my life BETTER???

9:03 a.m.

MONDAY

Dear #5667,

Greetings from A.D.I.S.D. I'm not allowed to go to my regular classes—I get to sit here in a small room at an even smaller desk with an even SMALLER pencil and write an incredibly small-minded essay on "How I Can Resolve My Conflicts Without Violence." Why don't they make Andrew write one on "Why I'm Such a Jerk"? His insulting me about my poem was as bad as me hitting him. Yeah, I know, the physical stuff always gets you in the most trouble, but doesn't anyone ever realize that words can hurt MORE than getting an English book in the nose?

Anyway, it doesn't matter, because I'm NOT going to write that essay. Even though my mom says I absolutely have to. She made me call Andrew at home this weekend and apologize. Then she sent me over to Mrs. Booth's house for half an hour while she talked to his mother. I guess she thought she should apologize more.

But I think I've apologized enough, and an essay isn't going to change my mind. Anyway, at least I have you to write to. I don't even care if you're reading these letters or not. At least this way it looks like I'm working on the essay. By the time they check to see what I've written, I'll have this letter stuffed in my pocket, and all I'll show them is a page on which I've written "Help. My name is Rapunzel, and I'm locked in a tower and can't get out. Please call 911. Reward offered for my safe return."

Too bad I can't call 911 about the bridge. Or offer a reward. But I've been thinking a lot about it. I think I should get the media involved. Did you ever wonder why Rapunzel didn't get the media involved in her case? Yeah, I know she's in the middle of nowhere, but there are birds that fly by now and then. She could get them to deliver a letter for her. She could write the police. Or one of those investigative TV shows. Or, at the very least, she could write a letter to the editor of the local fairy kingdom newspaper, protesting her plight and pleading for help.

Here's what she could say:

*Dear Kingdom Kronicle,*
*Have I got a story for you! Somewhere in*

*the Deep, Dark Woods, a beautiful girl has
been held against her will for years. This tragic
tale has everything: a dark family secret, a
spectacular tower setting, a mysterious young
heroine, and a possible shampoo endorsement
contract.*

*If you free her, she'll gladly sell you the
exclusive rights to her story, as well as
unlimited photos of her spectacular hair and
quaint abode. This could be the story of the
millennium! Don't wait!!*

*Yours most sincerely,
Rapunzel*

*P.S. Did I mention that my hair gets older but I
never do?*

Do you think a letter like that to our local paper
would work? I mean, if I didn't do it as a joke but
used my best persuasive writing powers, as Mr.
Stanley would say. I have to do something about
that bridge. It bothers me that one day soon a
place I've never even had a chance to see with my
dad will be GONE. And I don't

OK, I'm back. I had to pretend to start writing that essay. The vice-principal said she was going to call my mom. So I slowly wrote out the title, in fancy script, and underlined it three times. Then I had to make up stuff that I didn't mean.

But now no one's checking on me, because I'm supposed to be eating my lunch. So I can get back to the important stuff, like those letters to the editor that I mentioned. What do you think of this one?

*Dear Editor,*

*Are your readers aware that a great tragedy is about to befall the citizens of this fair county? I'm speaking, of course, about the imminent destruction of one of the last authentic swing bridges left in this area. The Breakers Point Railroad Bridge is of immense sentimental value to many of the area's longtime residents, who remember idyllic childhood days playing near its soaring steel arms. However, soon this nearly one-of-a-kind historic bridge will be doomed to execution by cruel dynamiting.*

*Will no one step forward and bear the cost*

*of gently transporting this beloved structure to*
*a safe resting place where it may spend the*
*rest of its days in peace, cared for and loved as*
*it was in its youth?*

*I'm but one concerned citizen, willing to*
*contribute what little I have ($10.23) to the*
*preservation of this bridge. Will others join me?*

*Sincerely and humbly yours,*
*A Loyal Reader*

*P.S. Long Live the Bridge!*

Or would this one be better?

*Dear Editor,*

*What can three-quarters of a million dollars*
*buy these days? A few million pieces of gum? A*
*half-dozen sports cars? One eighth of a house*
*for a movie star? Or a stay of execution for a*
*treasured piece of our community's history, the*
*Breakers Point Railroad Bridge?*

*Is three-quarters of a million dollars too*
*much to pay for the preservation of some of*
*the most precious memories our citizens have?*
*Indeed, how can one put a price on history*
*itself? Is it not priceless?*

*Please, please, join me in contributing what*

*you can to this most worthy cause. If we would*
*all give but a few dollars apiece, a great and*
*momentous tragedy would be averted.*
*Yours sincerely,*
*A Most Concerned Reader*

*P.S. Don't let the bridge become a faded*
*memory!*

I think BOTH of them. That way, the editor will
think there's more than one person worried about
the bridge.

Your favorite detainee,
Rapunzel

P.S. My birthday's this Saturday. In case you're
wondering what to get me, Three Wishes would be
nice. I'd use one to bring my dad home, one to
save the bridge, and one to have Andrew turned
into a two-headed frog.

Dear #5667,

I had that dream again about my dad. Only this time I didn't scream out loud. I kept TRYING to scream, but no sound would come out. Then the bridge turned into a tower and I was looking out of a tiny window and all I could see was the waterway down below. And then the tower started to get taller and taller, and I was shooting way up into the clouds and I couldn't breathe.

When I woke up, my pillow was over my face and my back was soaked with sweat.

Tired of the view from up here,
    Rapunzel

P.S. I wrote a letter to my dad, too. I'm going to ask my mom to take it to him. I told him I'd been writing you. And I lied and said you had been writing back.

P.P.S. Maybe you could, just once?

*Dear Dad,*

*I know you haven't forgotten, but Saturday's my birthday. Will you be able to send me a poem? If you can't, I'll understand. I know how hard they are to write, because I wrote one myself last week. It wound up getting me in a lot of trouble at school.*

*I've also been writing lots of letters— mostly to your friend at Box #5667—since you've been gone. I hope you don't mind, but I thought I should keep that friendship thing going for you. Especially since your friend might be able to help with the Evil Spell. The one that made you quit talking. The one that's keeping you locked up in the hospital. Your friend hasn't told me much yet, but I'm sure in his next letter he will.*

*I want to come visit you. Do you think you could talk to Mom about it?*

*Love,*

*Your favorite (and firstborn and best and only!) daughter*


*P.S. I've found a whole bunch of new words to stump you with when you get home. Here's a good one: "eudemon." I think that's what your friend at Box #5667 is.*

8:45 a.m.

TUESDAY

Dear #5667,

Greetings from Day Two of A.D.I.S.D. Yes, I'm still here. I thought I had that essay thing beat. I wrote a sincere first paragraph and a touching ending. I didn't think the vice-principal would read anything in between. But she did, and she was not amused by my freewriting about school bathrooms.

"Miss Brogan," she told me, her voice huffing like the Big Bad Wolf's, "THIS essay is NOT what I ASSIGNED. And UNTIL you COMPLETE it to MY satisfaction, you will NOT be going back to CLASS."

Or to my trial day in the GT classroom either, if they ever give me another chance. I think I've finally convinced everyone that I'm not a Smart Princess in disguise. I'm just a Dumb Beast.

9:52 a.m.

This detention thing is like Homework Club times ten. Worse, because I'm alone. At least in Homework Club there's that one decent girl that lets me borrow paper. She even helped me copy over one of my letters to the editor yesterday—in red ink, on different paper, so it would look like it came from a different person.

At least I'm getting to miss Computer Lab. Not that I don't like computers—I like them fine—but the ones in our lab are so lame you can't do anything fun on them like programming or building a Web page. We have to play these stupid keyboarding games, so we can learn how to type. Didn't anyone tell them that voice recognition is the way of the future? Personally, I like writing by hand anyway. Like these letters to you. Somehow they'd feel different if I were typing them. Why is that?

10:51 a.m.

I wonder what math opportunities I missed in class today. I wish we'd stop learning about how many square feet of tile it takes to cover a patio and do something interesting, like exploring how time works. I mean, the only time problems we ever get are how many minutes it takes for one train to get to a station I've never heard of. And there's always only one correct answer. As if time's always the same. It isn't.


10:54 a.m.


See? That was only three minutes. Three minutes that I sat here and did nothing. And it felt like FOREVER. How did Rapunzel stand it?


11:25 a.m.


"How I Can Resolve My Conflicts Without Violence"
    What a boring title. I think that's my problem. If I had a better title to work with, I could do it:
    "How I Can Look Like I Care When I Don't"
    "How I Can Be More Normal When I'm Not"
    "How I Can Can-Can with a Toucan from Canada"
    I think titles are important. Like "Goldilocks and the Three Bears." I mean, what does that tell you? I think this would be much better:

"The True Tale of a Girl Named Goldilocks, and Her Adventures with the Three Nameless Bears and Assorted Bowls of Porridge."

Or think about "Cinderella." That means nothing. It should be:

"The Complete Chronicles of Cinderella, from Fireplace to Fame, and All the Juicy Details in Between."

And "Jack and the Beanstalk"? How boring is that? But "How Jack Traded a Cow for Magic Beans and Met an Ogre Who Wanted to Grind His Bones, in Several Exciting Chapters, with Sound Effects!" Now that's a story you'd want to read.

12:02 p.m.

Maybe I should write that stupid essay. I could probably make up something thoughtful and contrite-sounding if I tried.

*Hitting someone with a book isn't a smart idea. In fairy tales, no one ever hits anyone with a book. The woodchopper does not use a book; he has an ax. The three little pigs don't use books; they have boiling water. Hansel and*

*Gretel forgot to take any books into the woods,*
*so they had to use a red-hot oven.*

I don't think the vice-principal will like this either.

12:40 p.m.

Okay. I'm so bored that I spent ten minutes watching the clock and saying "One Mississippi" each time the second hand clicked a space to see if time was mysteriously warped in this room like it is in Rapunzel's tower. But it's not. My hair and I are getting older at the exact same sluglike pace. And believe me, there's nothing to do in here besides feel your hair aging. So, even though I don't want to, I'm going to try to write that essay. I'm pretty sure it's what my dad would tell me to do. And it seems to be the only way out of this tower.

But I'm not sending you a copy. It's going to be bad enough having to write it once.

2:05 p.m.

I wrote the stupid essay. Finished it at 1:17 p.m. Now I'm back in class. The funny thing is, it's not much better being OUT than being IN, if you know what I mean.

Especially since I'm back in class with Andrew. Mr. Stanley moved us to opposite sides of the room, which is fine with me. Even if I do have to sit in the front row. The only thing is, Andrew is still bugging me. For one thing, when I turned around to look at the clock, he was staring at me. I whirled back around and tried not to think about him at all. But I did notice that his nose was still kind of bruised. Maybe he's worried I'm going to bean him with another book, all the way across six rows of desks.

Got to get out my deadly weapon (I mean my English book!) now,
      Rapunzel

P.S. When the vice-principal was reading my essay, I had time to write another letter to the editor. This one will be in green ink. In cursive.

*Dear Editor:*

*Perhaps you are unaware that one of the most esteemed poets in this region has recently completed a masterwork of poetry that* features the Breakers Point Bridge, which has unjustly been targeted for destruction (of which I know some of your readers have also written you!!!!). I shall be happy to reveal the name of this esteemed poet and share his wonderful work with you . . . if you publish this letter!!!!

> Sincerely yours,
> A Most Faithful Reader

P.S. I'm enclosing one of the poems from his manuscript so you can see how much this bridge means to him. He's very sick at the present time.

P.P.S. If you're interested, please call me at 555-950-9675. Leave a message.

9:27 a.m.

WEDNESDAY


Dear #5667,

Andrew's still acting weird. He tried to stop me before class, with a lame excuse about "needing to talk to me."

"I'm sorry," I said, as cool as sherbet, "I don't associate with known CREEPS." And I shifted my math book (which is even heavier than my English book!) in my arms a little, to remind his nose of our last encounter. He shut up pretty quick and went to his seat. But I can still feel him staring at me. Serves him right if he's feeling sorry now.

At least I'll be free of him on Friday, when he goes to GT and I don't.

Got to go. Mrs. Seisnek's giving me the laser eyes again.

Rapunzel

P.S. I gave my three letters to the editor to Mrs. Booth this morning. I told her it was for a school project. She said she'd drop them by the newspaper office for me. Which is great, because I'm running out of stamps. They have to publish at least ONE of my letters!

P.P.S. Don't they? Have to publish one, I mean?

3:40 p.m.

*Still* WEDNESDAY

I can't write much because I've got a lot of work to make up for the stuff I missed in class on Monday and Tuesday. For once, the Homework Witch won't be snapping her fingers at me because I don't look busy enough.

But I thought of one thing I forgot to tell you: Mrs. Booth gave me a big tin of Chinese fortune cookies when I saw her this morning. She said it was an early birthday present. And then she said she was going out of town for the weekend and asked if I'd look after her plants. She's going to pay me too!

I just sneaked a cookie from my backpack, and I'm eating it in little bitty nibbles so as not to attract the attention of the Homework Witch with my crunching. Here's my fortune:

*After a while, even the dog makes a*
*compromise with the cat.*

What does that mean? I don't even own a dog OR
a cat. The closest things I've got to a pet are the
dust bunnies that live in my closet.
  Still no reply from my dad.


  Rapunzel


P.S. Or from you. Do my letters have bad breath?
No one ever seems to answer them.

7:36 a.m.

THURSDAY *(on the bus)*

Dear #5667,

How could I be so dumb? A reporter called early this morning, before I got on the bus (luckily, my mom was still in the shower), but since I didn't answer the phone in my fake grown-up voice, she realized how old I am. She said she couldn't interview me without my parents' permission. When I said that the story wasn't about me anyway, that the poet was my dad, she said OK, then let me talk to your dad. Of course, then I had to say he wasn't home and I didn't know when he would be. And then she said it wouldn't be much of a story without talking to the poet himself, and when I tried to say that his poems could speak for him, she said no, they couldn't, because she couldn't print any of his poems without copyright permission.

I asked her if she could do a general story on the bridge and its imminent destruction, and she said, sure, she'd pass it on to the news desk, but that she did "human interest features," and without a human, the story wasn't likely to get anywhere. She did leave me her number, in case things changed, but she didn't sound real hopeful.

I need a new plan.

Rapunzel

P.S. You think you can make me stop writing you by not writing back, don't you? Well, it isn't going to work. I've read lots of fairy tales, and in all of them, the heroine NEVER gives up.

Dear #5667,

I can't believe it. Andrew's such a creep. Look at the note he handed me in math:

> *I'm sorry I made fun of your poem.*
> *I didn't know about your dad and that bridge.*
>    *Andrew*
> *P.S. I hope he gets better soon.*

What does he mean about my dad and "that bridge"? How does Andrew know about my dad's poems and his not-yet-published book?


11:30 a.m.

I wrote Andrew back and dropped the note on his desk as I walked to the pencil sharpener:

*My dad's poems are wonderful. Better than wonderful—they're spectacular. And since when do you care about what books my dad gets published?*

11:37 a.m.

Then the bell rang for lunch, and I tried to avoid him as we were all getting up, but he shoved this note at me anyway:

*I don't know anything about your dad's books. I meant about how they found him on that old swing bridge. Your mom told my mom.*
     *You could talk to Ms. Trey if you wanted to. I think she knows too.*

What a liar. I'm going to see Ms. Trey right now. Before I chase Andrew down in the lunchroom and break his head open with my math book.

Ms. Trey wasn't in her office. So I went to the library instead of to lunch and used the Internet. I did a search on my dad's name and nothing unusual came up. Then I did a search on the bridge and nothing except some pictures and the original notice in the paper came up. If someone had found my dad up on that bridge, wouldn't it have been in the news? Wouldn't that reporter have known about it when I talked to her this morning? So Andrew's wrong, wrong, wrong. He's just trying to get back at me for hitting him.

I wish I knew how to put a curse on him, because I'd do it right now. I'd wish that every time he opened his mouth, black wiggly snakes and warty toads would spill out of it. I'd wish that every hair on his head would catch on fire, one at a time, and burn like those trick birthday candles that never go out. I'd wish his real name was Rumplestiltskin, and that everybody in school knew it.

Maybe Mrs. Booth will know the truth. She's going out of town tomorrow, but I can ask her tonight when she shows me how to take care of the plants. But first I have to get through the rest of class. And then, 135 minutes of Homework Club.

1:00 a.m.

THURSDAY, *changed into*
*FRIDAY*

I asked Mrs. Booth. I showed her the note from
Andrew. She gave me a big hug and said, "Honey,
you have to talk to your mom about this, not
me."

But my mom had five babies to help deliver
tonight. And when she got home, she headed
straight to the bathtub. While she was in there, I
called the hospital and asked to speak to my dad.
They wouldn't let me.

What if Andrew isn't lying? I can't sleep thinking about it.

I have to find out.


Rapunzel


P.S. I'm not writing you anymore. What's the
point?

# Part Two

><

*(In Which Rapunzel
Seeks a Happy Ending)*

1:58 p.m.

FRIDAY


Dear #5667,

I said I wasn't writing you anymore, but I changed my mind. Don't think I'm not still mad at you, though, because I definitely AM. You could've helped my dad and you didn't. You could've told me the truth and you didn't. It's just that there isn't anyone I want to talk to in here, and I have to put my thoughts someplace. Because now I'm locked up for real.

Let me back up a little. Rewind to this morning.

After what Andrew said, I couldn't face him at school. I had to figure out the truth. So I went out the door like I was going to the school bus, but instead I took the key Mrs. Booth had given us and hid out at her house until my mom left for work. She's working a double shift today so she can be off on my birthday tomorrow. Then I came back home and called that reporter again. I told her I was working on a school project, and was researching the bridge on my own.

"Do you know if anything bad ever happened there?" I asked.

"Bad?" she said. "Like a crime?"

"Not exactly," I said. She couldn't see me, so I closed my eyes and imagined I was looking at the stars from my dad's shoulders. The flashlight was off and he was counting to ten, slowly. "Like if a person was up on that bridge, would that be in the newspaper?"

"Yes and no," she said. "We do a weekly police blotter report. But there are no names. You could probably find out if and when something like that happened, but not who."

My dad was still counting. FIVE . . . SIX . . . SEVEN . . .

"Can you look up a date from last month?" I asked. My voice wavered even though I willed it not to.

There was a pause on the other end of the line.

"Why do you want to know this?"

EIGHT . . . NINE . . . I kept my eyes closed and made my voice light and carefree. "Oh, you know, my teacher likes us to be specific when we are writing . . . you know, use lots of details. He hates it when we don't use dates and stuff."

"So does my editor," she said with a chuckle.

"Hang on and I'll check the records."

I opened my eyes so I could see my watch. She was gone three minutes and seventeen seconds.

"Yes," she said. "There was an incident last month. A male, age forty-two. A jumper. The police noticed him on a routine patrol and talked him down. That's all the information I have."

"Thank you," I said.

## TEN . . .
## THINGS THAT HAPPENED AFTER THAT

1. I hung up the phone.
2. I got the directions the lady at the government office had given me to the bridge and I pulled out my grandpa's map.
3. I figured out what city bus stop was closest to that bridge.
4. I rode the bus.
5. I hiked two miles after I got off the bus.
6. I got lost three times.
7. I found the bridge. It looked just like my dad had described, except he hadn't mentioned the smelly muck of decaying leaves that surrounded it.
8. I sloshed through the gross brownish green

gunk (worse than that snot I wrote about)
and climbed over a torn piece of metal
fence. Of course I saw the sign that said No
Trespassing, but I didn't figure anyone would
care because the bridge was coming down
anyway.

9. I found a dry piece of rock to perch on and
sat near the bridge for a long time, maybe
two hours, trying to understand why Evil
Spells exist and wondering why nobody
thinks I'm brave enough to know the truth
about them. I tried to figure out how my dad
could've tried to leave me.

10. How could my dad, who's smart and funny,
and one of the best people of any millennium,
have gone up there on that bridge and tried
to jump off? What kind of dad does that?????

Then the police arrived. I guess they patrol pretty
regularly. They made me climb back over the
fence and away from the bridge, and they gave
me a lecture about safety and trespassing, and I
guess they would've just given me a ride home
except that I wouldn't tell them my name.

If I'd told them, I might not be in this detention
place. But for some reason, all I could say when

they asked me my name was "Rapunzel." That's why I'm here. And I'm not going home because there's no one there who cared enough to tell me the truth.

Yours most sincerely,
    Rapunzel for Real

P.S. I'm not sure they'll let me mail this. Not that I'd send it to you anyway. You never answer me, and I guess you aren't going to start now.

3:02 p.m.

Dear #5667,

It has been one hour, four minutes, and two seconds since the last time I wrote you. But don't worry; I can't keep up this pace. For one thing, this is my last piece of paper. They won't give me any more unless I tell them my real name. Why can't my real name be Rapunzel? Celebrities name their kids crazy things, like Moonflower or Bingo. Why can't I be Rapunzel?

I don't even know why I'm writing this. I don't have anywhere to send it to, even if they did let me have a stamp, which they won't. It's like I'm talking to myself. I wonder if Rapunzel talked to herself to keep from going crazy up there in that tower alone. The story goes that she sang a lot, and that's what the prince heard and how he came to rescue her, but I bet she talked up a storm too:

"Guess what? I've got the best news! I think my hair grew another inch. See, now I can wind it around my big toe!"

"Oh, Rapunzel—that's amazing! You're too much, girl!"

Got to go . . . I think they found a social worker. She's swooping this way. . . .

5:22 p.m.

I was wrong . . . that wasn't the social worker . . . it was somebody's mother, who swooped right on by me. The real social worker turned out to be a woman named Mrs. Dunn who wears purple eye shadow and is round as a cupcake. She wouldn't be bad as a kindergarten teacher, but she's way too soft to work with older kids. I got more paper out of her right away, in exchange for coughing up my name and phone number.

Except, of course, I gave her a fake name and Mrs. Booth's number. She can leave lots of messages for "Ashley Booth's mother" and all I have to do when I get home is take the key Mrs. Booth left for us to water her plants and erase all those messages.

The ever clever,

Rapunzel

P.S. Time served (so far): three hours and twenty-four minutes. How long can I hold out????

P.P.S. Look what I've been working on with the paper she gave me.

125

# THE TRUE STORY OF RAPUNZEL
## (BY NONE OTHER THAN HERSELF)

"Does she sing?" asked the dwarf, without looking up. His face was as round and rough as a dragon's egg, and nearly as pink. His red-feathered pen was poised over the form in front of him.

"Like a nightingale," said the witch, and she poked Rapunzel in the ribs. "Go ahead, sweetie, chirp a few bars. . . ."

"La," sang Rapunzel. "La, la, laaaaaa, laaaaaaaaah!" The dwarf's inkpot quivered as if it were about to shatter. And it was dragonproof glass.

"Stop! Stop!" said the dwarf. "You sound more like a gale than a nightingale!"

He looked at the chart he had been laboring over. There was a single line of red marks going down one side of the page, every one of them in the NO column.

"Let me see. She doesn't sing; she doesn't dance; she doesn't have beautiful silky hair; she doesn't have exquisite manners; she doesn't know a single wealthy prince; she doesn't get good grades; and she's been known to assault boys with large books. And why exactly do you think there's a place for her here at Tower Estates?" The dwarf looked up, his pudgy nose twitching from side to side as if he were trying to sniff the answer out of thin air.

"She writes letters," said the witch. "Lots of them!"

"I see," said the dwarf. His pen hovered near the block marked OTHER. "And what kind of letters does she write? Sincere notes of apology? Effusive expressions of thankfulness? Compassionate words of sympathy?"

"Oh no," said Rapunzel. "Mostly, I write letters that no one ever answers." She smiled to herself, knowing she had foiled the witch's scheme to leave her at Tower Estates and live off the income of her labor.

"Perfect!" cried the dwarf. "Why didn't you say so before?"

He scrawled a few words on his form, then folded it in thirds and stamped it with a large black image of a tower.

"We have just the place for her in Tower Eighty-two. There, at the edge of the forest. The corner room with the owl-shaped water stain and the cracked left window." He handed the witch a large key. "Don't forget to lock her in!" he said cheerfully.

"Wait!" said Rapunzel as the witch dragged her off. "I don't understand. Why are you keeping me here?"

"You'll be working for Fairy Tale Incorporated's complaint department," called the dwarf as he happily filed her stamped form in a large cabinet marked New Arrivals. "You wouldn't believe how many people try to write back after the company's already answered their complaint once. Now, with you, we'll be rid of them after only one reply!"

He waved his feathered pen at them. "Watch out for the spiders! And mind the poison ivy growing round the doorknob!"

So it was that Rapunzel found herself locked high in Tower 82, alone except for the mountains of complaint letters that were delivered to her each day, along with a daily ration of gruel, brackish water, and cheap typing paper. To her horror, she discovered that her replies were expected to be composed on an ancient device called a typewriter, which besides having keys that stuck when it rained, was unbelievably loud and prone to leaving globs of ink on her pages.

Worse still were the people she was ordered to correspond with. People who complained that the plot of "The Three Little Pigs" was too gruesome. People who thought "Goldilocks and the Three Bears" sent the wrong message to would-be juvenile trespassers. People who pointed out "seven-league boots" were a scientific impossibility, especially when worn by a cat. People who objected to "Little Red Riding Hood" because the grandmother was portrayed as a weak and helpless senior citizen. People who thought "Cinderella" promoted unhealthy high-heel wearing. But especially, people who demanded that stories be rewritten with happier endings.

Rapunzel had to reply to all of them. It was part of her job. If a customer wrote and said he objected to the "anti-sleep message" of "Sleeping Beauty," Rapunzel could send off a quick "Too bad!!!" letter and that was that. But if the customer used the Magic Words—"I demand a Happy Ending"—then Rapunzel was stuck, bound by the spell of her captivity, to deliver a new, revised version. If she didn't—if she failed ONCE in the three-year term of her captivity to provide a Happy

Ending—then the witch would own her forever.

It was tough, demanding work, making everything turn out happily for everybody in a story. At first, Rapunzel didn't think she'd ever be able to do it. How much easier this would be, she thought as she sat by her teeny-tiny window, if a prince were out there, with a sack full of Happy Endings, waiting to toss one up to me whenever I needed it.

But soon she discovered that if she developed a workable Happy Ending for one story, she could simply reuse it when the next, similar complaint came in. Before long, she had a new, totally cheerful version of nearly every traditional fairy tale, and was able to answer most complaints with a simple form letter. The months crept by until one morning, the very day before her captivity was due to end, Rapunzel received a disturbing letter . . .

TO BE CONTINUED!!!

6:31 p.m.

FRIDAY

Dear #5667,

I decided that I'm NOT staying here any longer. For one thing, I'm getting hungry, and I don't think they'll be serving me egg rolls. For another, Mrs. Dunn came back and practically tried to smother me. She's "SOOO concerned" that no one's answering the phone at my house.

The problem is, plotting an escape's a lot harder than plotting a story. One thing I can't figure out is how to get out of here without giving them my name. I don't like the thought of leaving my name here—it's like leaving part of myself for them to use against me. Like the real Rapunzel. The witch cut off her hair, and then used it against her.

What's wrong with me? Now all I can think of is how I'm like a silly fairy-tale character? As if that were really me. Except look at the facts. I can't save the bridge from being blown up. I can't help my dad get better. I can't get Andrew to leave me alone. I can't even pass English. I might as well BE Rapunzel, locked in a tower, for all the good I'm doing. Maybe it would be better if I did my homework the "right" way, if I smiled nicely at Andrew, if I called the Evil Spell "C.D." like my mom wants me to, and if I didn't care at all about a bridge that's surrounded by muck and weeds.

But I can't. There's a little stubborn part of myself that keeps growing my wild, willful hair again no matter how many times the witch (or Andrew or my teachers or this social worker or even my dad) cuts it off.

Talk to you later,
    Rapunzel

P.S. Part Two will have to wait. I'm going to try to get out of here. . . .

8:06 p.m.

*Still* FRIDAY

Dear #5667,

I'm still here. I tried pulling the fire alarm, but I guess that plot has been used before, because it didn't cause nearly the chaos I needed it to. The only good thing is that I don't think they know it was me who started the fire drill. Otherwise, I wouldn't still have this paper to write on. I may not have it for long anyway if Mrs. Dunn wises up about the fake phone number.

Rapunzel (who has now been here over SIX STUPID HOURS!!)

P.S. Looks like I've got time for Part Two after all. I think I can fit it on this paper if I write really, really small.

# THE TRUE STORY OF RAPUNZEL

## (FROM WHERE I LEFT OFF)

It was a letter that she didn't know how to answer:

*Dear Complaint Department,*
    *Please help me. I've been cursed!*
    *You see, a few days ago, when I opened my front door, I discovered that someone—in the middle of the night—had left a package on my front steps. When I opened the mysterious parcel, I found nothing but the first few pages of a story I had never heard before. Unable to stop myself, I read the pages, thereby triggering the curse. For at the end of this seemingly innocent manuscript was a Magic Spell. You'll see what I mean when you read it!*
    *I'm sure this package was sent to me by mistake, and I've written Fairy Tale, Incorporated several times about their error. I asked them to come pick up the package immediately. I even tried to mail it back to them, but the story simply reappeared on my doorstep the next day.*
    *You don't know what it's like having this*

*story inside my head. You must help me! I*
*demand a Happy Ending!*
    *Wailing with sorrow,*
        *A most unhappy customer*

*P.S. I enclose the cursed story for your*
*repair.*

Rapunzel groaned. It was bad enough trying to make Happy Endings for the stories she already was familiar with. But to write one for a totally new story? With great trepidation and much nail-biting, she began to read the enclosed story.

## THE RUBY APPLE
### A Tale of Love, Battle, and True Courage

Once upon a time, in a kingdom far away, there was a king who had but one daughter. Since he had no other family, his daughter was precious to him, and he always spent as much time as he could with her (and probably more time than he ought to have, considering the precarious state of his tiny kingdom's poorly defended border).

One day, news came that his enemies were plotting an invasion. War was imminent. Sadly, the king went to take leave of his beloved daughter. He took with him the largest, most perfect, and utterly beautiful apple from his royal orchard.

"This apple that I give you is my heart," said the king to his daughter. "Keep it safe for me until I return. I'll be home as soon as I win this war." Then he took his place at the head of his army and rode to defend his borders.

But his daughter did not understand. How could she keep this apple, which he called his heart, safe? If she ate it, it would be destroyed. If she didn't eat it, it would grow rotten and decay. How could she preserve it? Freeze it in a block of ice? That would ruin the taste. Dry it out? That would cause it to lose its shape and color.

"What am I to do?" she cried. "There's no telling how long the war will last, and surely this apple will shrivel and rot before my father can return home!"

But there was no one to give her counsel, so she did the best she could. She kept the apple out of the sun, in her pocket during the day and under her pillow at night. She sprinkled it with water each morning, and polished it, and took as loving care of it as if it were her own flesh.

But despite her efforts, one day she felt a soft bruise on its skin, and a tiny wrinkle appeared near its slender stem. It was beginning to rot. And the news from the war was not good. The army was bitterly engaged in a protracted defense of the northern pass, and her father wouldn't be home for many months. She couldn't bear it.

"If I don't protect this apple," she cried, "my father will surely die in the war! Whatever shall I do?"

*And there the story ended, except for the curse, which read:*

SOMEWHERE LIES A HAPPY ENDING TO THIS TALE.
FIND THE WORDS, OR
FOREVER HEAR SORROW'S WAIL.

Rapunzel pulled at her hair. Hard. That helped her think. (It didn't hurt much because her hair was very short, due to safety precautions taken after one of the Tower Estates residents had escaped using her long hair and a clever prince with hairdresser training.) But no matter how hard she pulled or twisted or groaned, she couldn't think of a way to give the customer a Happy Ending for her story.

Beside herself with despair at the thought of being locked in her tower for life, Rapunzel threw her typewriter out her teeny-tiny window. Actually, the window wasn't quite big enough for her to throw it out all at once, so she began to do it piece by piece. First keys Q, Z, and X, which she hardly used anyway. Then, as she was preparing to throw out the Shift key and abandon capital letters forever, she heard a voice calling out to her, below her window. Could it be the Prince of Happy Endings?

## TO BE CONTINUED!!!!

*About* 11:00 p.m. *I think*
FRIDAY


A Virtual Letter to #5667:

They wouldn't give me any more paper. But it wouldn't matter anyway, because the lights are out and I don't have my flashlight, so I'm writing this letter to you in the dark, in my head.

I hate it here. This place has a funny smell, like a school mixed with a hospital mixed with a little bit of the inside of a Dumpster. And the bed has scratchy sheets, and a pillow so limp you can't even hug it.

There's nothing to do but lie here and try to think of an ending to my story. Except I can't think of one. All I can think about is my dad, up there on that bridge. Why? Why did he do that? And will he try to do it again? I'm afraid to close my eyes because if I do I might see him falling. And then I might start falling, like you do in dreams, only what if, this time, it's real?

I guess that's why Mom didn't tell me what happened. Only it's no good, not telling, because that's just like blowing up the bridge. Even after it's gone, what people did there, both good and bad, will still be real.

And then there's you. I've written you a whole lot of letters, and you haven't answered a single one. Does that mean you've gone and jumped off a bridge too? Does that mean I'm crazy for still writing you, here in my head in the dark? Who are you?

The sleepless,
Rapunzel

P.S. I'm imagining my flashlight is shining on me, safely circling me in its mighty beam.

7:07 a.m.

SATURDAY *(My birthday,*
*remember? Like you care)*

Dear #5667,

I am rescued. Except I think that means I'm in more trouble than ever.

My mom's on her way. She discovered I was missing when she got home from work late last night and contacted the police. I guess it took them the whole night to figure out that it was me who was missing, not "Ashley Booth."

She called here about five minutes ago. I think she wanted to yell at me, but she was crying so she couldn't. And I lost my head for a second, and the words came tumbling out of my mouth, like frogs and toads.

"I know about Dad and the bridge, Mom. And you know how I found out? ANDREW! How does Andrew know something about my OWN DAD that I don't? Why did you tell his mom? Why did you tell Ms. Trey at school? Did you tell Mrs. Booth too? Did you tell the mailman?" The words were jumping out of my mouth so fast that I could hardly breathe. "Did you tell the waitress at the Happy Palace? Did you tell all of MRS. BOOTH'S PLANTS?" I took one more deep breath and the last toad hopped out.

I yelled, "AND NOT ME?????"

And then I slammed down the phone. Because I was crying too. Mrs. Dunn gave me a whole stack of writing paper after that.

I hope they didn't tell my mom that I was at the bridge, but I guess they did. I'm in big trouble.

Your favorite criminal,
    Rapunzel

P.S. Can you think of a Happy Ending for this?

7:20 a.m.

*Still* SATURDAY


Dear #5667,

I didn't wait to be rescued. They stopped watching me as closely after they knew my mom was coming, so I was able to stuff my pen and paper in my back pocket, hide my map under my shirt, and slip out the door during breakfast. No ropes, no levers, no pulleys. Just a quick, quiet rescue. I walked to the corner, got on a bus headed in the right direction, and pulled out my map again. I'm sure I can figure out which stop to get off at.

I need to find the ending for my story. I need to see what's beyond my tower. Once my mom gets here, I'll never have another chance. So I'm going back to the bridge. I need to stop falling and start climbing.

Got to go,
     Rapunzel

P.S. Don't worry about me.

Dear #5667,

I did it. I found the bridge again. It wasn't as hard this time because I knew where I was going. I had paid attention when they drove me in the police car from the bridge to the detention center. Mom says I'm the only one in the family with any sense of direction. I always have to read maps for her and keep her from getting lost. And my dad's worse. He can remember what color a tree was last year in the fall, and describe it perfectly, but he can't tell you how to find it again.

The second thing I had to do was make a plan for how I was going to get up there. The end of the bridge was blocked off with barbed wire, so the only way to get on it was to wade into the cold brown water and crawl up one of the pilings, which were towers of crumbling concrete as far as I could tell. There wasn't much to hold on to, just cracks, black with age, and random spikes of rusty metal, totally covered with bird poop. I had to fold my paper inside my map and leave it on the shore, but my pen went up with me. I could feel it jabbing my leg as I climbed.

I kept thinking, the whole time I was struggling up, about those dreams I had. The ones with my dad in the box, and water pouring in. The ones with me in the tower with the teeny-tiny window. It was like those dreams were movies, playing over and over in my head. Except I was IN the movie, and it was ME whose legs were shaking so hard that I thought I'd suddenly contracted a weird disease that disconnects your muscles from your brain.

And everything—the water, the trees, the sound of cars on the road far behind me—seemed to fade out until there was nothing but me and my breath going in and out in a roaring rhythm. And all the way up, I was carrying inside me, cutting into my chest, this jagged black rock of Fear.

The worst part was getting from the piling onto the bridge itself. I realized after I got near the top of the piling that I was going to have to let go with one hand so that I could reach up for the railing. I wrapped my legs as tightly as I could around the post, and smashed my cheek against the concrete. Then I closed my eyes and stretched up for the bridge above me. My hand was circling, round and round. There was nothing to hold on to. And I knew, suddenly, that Fear was right this time. I shouldn't be up here.

But I was just as scared to go down as I was to go up. It was Into the Woods either way. I'm a fortune, I thought, the crazy thought zinging through my head. I'm a folded-up piece of the future that's about to drop into the Mason jar and be lost. *You will inherit riches! You will be crowned Queen! You will die covered in bird poop!*

Or, I thought, *You will get up there on that bridge. You will do what you came to do.*

I tensed my legs and shot upward with all my strength, scraping the skin off my stomach where my shirt had come untucked. My cheek stung, too, from under my eye to my lip, and my right shoe came off, bouncing with a thunk into the muddy water below.

But my fingers were hooked on the rail. I pulled my body upward, inching with my legs until I could get my other hand up too. Then I swung one foot up, and rolled onto the top of the bridge.

Once I was there, I was still scared, but the view helped. It was better than anything Rapunzel ever saw from her tower. Of course, it wasn't anywhere near as high as the Statue of Liberty, at least not on the flat railroad track part. I didn't go up on the railings above. I'm not that dumb. But unlike the Statue of Liberty view, I didn't peek with one eye open for just two seconds. I used both my eyes, and all my heart, for as long as I could stand it.

I could see patterns of light in the water, and how the river changed color as it got deeper. I could see the wispy tops of trees, swaying as if they were bowing in my direction and waving their last few golden leaves. I could see the edge of the earth, and I felt as if the whole bridge was built as a throne for me to survey my kingdom.

I pulled my pen from my pocket, held it tightly in my fingers, and thought about those words my dad wrote when he was under the Evil Spell: "You must be willing to have your heart broken in order to live."

I didn't think I knew what that meant. But now maybe I do. It broke my heart to see my dad curled up in his red chair, crying. It broke my heart when Andrew read my poem out loud and made fun of it. It broke my heart when I heard the reporter tell me about my dad and this bridge.

But if you asked me whether I'd do it again, I would. I'd hug my dad in his chair; I'd write my poem; and I'd hear the truth about this bridge. I'd even write my letters to you all over again, even though you never wrote me back. Because otherwise, I'd just be a silly princess, waiting for rescue. I wouldn't have known that from the top of this tower I have a pretty good view. I think that's what the Evil Spell does—it keeps you from seeing anything but the walls of your tower.

Maybe I shouldn't have done it. Climbed the bridge. But I did. And after I sat there a while, I took my pen and wrote my poem—you know, the one Andrew laughed at—on the side of one of the steel posts. Kind of stupid, I know, but it made me feel better, countering one Evil Spell with a Good Spell of my own.

Only it's not going to last because once they blow up that bridge, there goes my poem too. And I know that will break my heart again. But I am willing to live with it.

After that, I climbed down and walked to the nearest convenience store and I called my mom on her cell phone. That was scarier than going up on the bridge.

Yours truly,
Rapunzel

P.S. It's very hard, rescuing yourself.

Dear #5667,

I'm writing this on the way home. My mom's so upset she won't even talk to me while she's driving. She says she'll have a wreck if she does.

"Your face—you're bleeding," was the first thing she said. Then, "Your feet—they're soaking wet! And what happened to your shoe?"

"Can we go home, Mom?" I said. "I'm hungry."

She took me by the arms. "Do you know how worried I was about you? And when I got to the center and you weren't there and they didn't know . . ." She quit talking and pulled me into a hug. She was still in her nurse's uniform, and she smelled more like sweat than her usual soap.

We got into the car. She took a folded piece of blue paper from her purse.

"I was going to put this beside your plate this morning," she said. "Happy Birthday." She handed me a letter from Dad.

"I went to the bridge, Mom," I said.

"I know," she said. "Now don't talk anymore. I have to drive."

That's all for today,
    Rapunzel

P.S. I can't wait for my flashlight to read it. I have to open it now.

*Dear Cadence,*

*Your mother brought me your letter. I'm sorry it took me so long to write you back, but I haven't been well enough to write before now. I was surprised to hear that you've been writing to Box #5667, although I shouldn't have been, knowing you as I do.*

*I don't know of any easy way to say this, dear Cadence, but there's no person who eagerly checks #5667 for your letters. No kind and understanding friend who will gladly write you back and give you honest and brilliant advice, no matter how much you might have wished it. At least there wasn't for me.*

*I wrote to that box because it was the only way I could learn how to listen to myself. I felt safe mailing my thoughts away to it, much safer than if I'd kept them in a diary. Then, every few months, I'd go down to the post office and collect my letters, go off by myself, and listen to my life.*

*This has been especially true this past year, since I've been suffering from depression again. I don't know how much you know about this illness, but I've fought it all my life, and it seems as if it will always be with me. I don't know how to describe it except to say that it's like being locked in a dark room, and you've forgotten your name, why you're there, where the door is, even that the outside world exists. You know you should get up and look for a way out, but you've forgotten the magic words that bring the light. It is, indeed, as you named it in your letter, an Evil Spell, and I hope you'll forgive me for what I tried to do under its enchantment.*

*Will you want to keep writing to this box now that you know its secret? I don't know. I hope you'll at least go to the post office and get back the letters you sent to its care. The key is in my desk, in the little drawer at the top right-hand corner. See what you had to say when you thought there was someone important listening. Someone important was.*

*Please try not to worry about me. I'm doing my best to get well.*

*Dad*

*P.S. Great word you sent me. Eudemon. Is that from my dictionary? What does it mean?*

12:01 a.m.

SUNDAY

*(My birthday is over.)*

Dear Nobody,

So this whole thing with you was a fraud. You're a nothing. A nobody. And I wrote to you like you were the greatest thing since canned peaches.

At least it explains why you never wrote me back, and it wasn't because you didn't like me.

This is too strange,
Rapunzel

P.S. Another weird thing is, I've gotten used to talking to myself. Look, I'm still doing it!

10:22 a.m.
MONDAY

Dear Nobody,

I don't know which was worse, being locked up in that detention center or being locked up here at home. I was grounded all day yesterday. My mom wouldn't even let me go alone next door to water Mrs. Booth's plants. She went with me.

And today, now that Mrs. Booth's back, she asked her to stay over here with me while she went to school to talk to Ms. Trey about me and my absence on Friday. I'm under strict orders not to leave my room except to eat lunch. Which will be onion soup, because I can smell Mrs. Booth cooking it. Mom's going to call me on her cell phone every hour to make sure I'm still here.

More later,
Rapunzel

P.S. Why does she think I feel like running away again? Once was enough.

Dear Nobody,

What I have to tell you is this: My mom's letting me come with her to see my dad. I guess when she met with Ms. Trey at the school, Ms. Trey convinced her it would be a good thing. He's staying at a place called the Duncan Center for Residential Treatment Programs. He went there after he left the regular hospital, and it's for people with hard-to-cure Evil Spells, like him.

I don't know what else my mom and Ms. Trey talked about, but my mom was a lot less mad at me when she got back from the school. Not that she ungrounded me or anything. But she did say she was sorry that I found out about my dad and the bridge from Andrew.

"I didn't want you to be afraid," she said. "I didn't want you to think Dad didn't love you . . . because he . . . because of the . . ."

"Because of the Evil Spell," I finished for her.

"But I know that. And I want to see Dad as soon as I can."

So I get to see my dad after school tomorrow. If I live through school, that is. I don't want to go back, but my mom says I have to. And she says I have to give the GT program on Fridays a chance. Even if Andrew's in it. I tried to tell her that test was probably a big mistake. But she wouldn't listen.

"You need to be challenged, honey," she said. "You need to DO something with that imagination of yours."

And Mrs. Booth backed her up. "Your Grandpa," she said, "he was always learning, up until the end. I taught him how to grow herbs. He taught me how to read a map. The only thing he could never figure out was how to make my onion soup." She laughed. "But I don't think he tried very hard."

"But the GT program doesn't teach you how to make soup," I said. "And what if I don't fit in there?"

"Oh, you'll be fine," said Mrs. Booth. "You're as strong an onion as I've seen in quite a long time."

At least I get to skip Homework Club tomorrow.

Yours truly,
Rapunzel

P.S. I still can't think of a way to end that story I started. It's starting to bug me.

P.P.S. I'm working on another letter to bring to my dad.

Dear Dad,

I'm trying to understand about you and the Evil Spell, but right now I can't. Nothing makes sense to me and I don't know how to fix anything. All I have is questions. Like, here's one:

Do you remember when I was eight, when I found out my name was in your big dictionary? Before that I didn't know it was a real word. Ever since then, I look for my name in all sorts of places. Like the other day at the post office, I looked for it in the ZIP code book. (Not there!)

Anyway, I looked up my name in your dictionary again:

> Cadence: 1) balanced, rhythmic flow, as of
> poetry or oratory. 2) The measure of beat of
> movement, as in dancing or marching. 3)
> Music: a progression of chords moving to a
> harmonic close or point of rest.

And then there was a part that I'd never noticed before. About where the word . . . and my name . . . came from:

*Middle English from Old French, from Old Italian "cadenza," from "cadere," to fall or to die, from Latin. . . ."*

That's kind of like having a curse for a name, don't you think? Why did you name me that?

Wondering,
    Rapunzel

P.S. You see that I've been using a new name since you've been gone.

6:03 p.m.
TUESDAY


Dear #5667,

It was scary seeing my dad. He was pale and skinny, and even though he was dressed in normal clothes, they didn't fit him anymore. He seemed tired, too, as if each time he talked, it was an effort to get the words out. But he seemed glad I was there, and I gave him my letter, and he promised to write back.

I didn't mention me getting caught at the bridge, or his poems coming back from the publisher, or my troubles at school. I figured my mom could tell him all that if she wanted to. What I wanted to talk to him about was WHY. Why he was up there on the bridge. But I couldn't. I couldn't even be mad at him. He looked small.

On the way home, my mom said he'd be able to come home soon. The doctors are pretty sure his new medications are finally working.

More later,
    Rapunzel

P.S. He asked me if I'd gotten my letters back from the post office yet. I told him no, but that I was still writing you anyway. He seemed happy about that.

P.P.S. I decided that I AM going to keep on writing you, even if you are just me in disguise. After all, if I can't talk to myself, who can I talk to?

10:44 a.m.
THURSDAY


Dear #5667,

I'm in science class, and I'm supposed to be taking notes on the <u>What Makes Our Weather?</u> video we are watching, but I can't. I keep thinking about all my letters, waiting for me in Dad's box. The post office called yesterday and left a message about it. I guess because of me, the box is overflowing. If someone doesn't go down there soon and clear it out, they said, they will have to suspend his service.

   I'm going to ask Mom if she'll take me down there this Saturday.


   Got to go now,
         Rapunzel


P.S. Do you think it's safe to send this? One more letter and you might EXPLODE!!!!

4:24 p.m.

FRIDAY


Dear #5667,

Well, I'm officially in the GT program. At least until
the next grading period. If I don't fail any classes, I
can stay in. If I want to. I'm not sure I want to yet.

THE THINGS I LIKE ABOUT GT:
1. The teacher. Her name's Ms. Kobroniewski,
   but we can call her Ms. K if we want. She's
   short, with red wispy hair, and she turns her
   head to the side a lot, like an owl. The best
   thing about her is that she talks to us like we
   are real people.
2. Independent study. We get to pick a topic we
   are interested in and do a whole project on it.
   Anything at all. Not what the teacher wants us
   to learn about. What WE want to know.

THE THINGS I DON'T LIKE ABOUT GT:
1. Andrew, of course. But at least I don't have to
   sit by him.

2. Makeup work. We have to make up everything we miss in our regular classes. Even if it's stuff we already knew BEFORE they taught it. That's what I'm doing in Homework Club today.

THE THINGS I'M NOT SURE IF I LIKE YET OR NOT:
1. The other people in the class. Some of them are totally nerdy, and some of them look completely normal, but all of them seem to be sure they belong there.
2. Not being bored. Well, yeah, I didn't like being bored all the time in class, but it did give me lots of time to do other stuff, like write letters. I couldn't write you in class today. And there's NO time to work on my story either. Not that I've got any good ideas for it yet. Do you think I've stopped being able to think up good stuff?

That's it for now,
    Rapunzel

P.S. I could do my independent study on Evil Spells. Or do you think anyone would be interested?

11:59 p.m.

FRIDAY *night*


Dear Dad,

Thanks for writing back. Mom says I can come see
you again whenever she goes. So I guess I could
tell you this in person. But I'm afraid I'll forget
exactly how I was going to say the words when it
comes time to say them, so I want to write them
down, to be sure.

I went back and used your dictionary again, like
you said. You're right. There ARE good words
related to my name. I found: "cascade," "chance,"
and "chute." There's even "deciduous" (as in
falling leaves, which there are piles of in the back-
yard. Wait until you get home and see them.).

Of course, I can't say that I'm thrilled that my
name's also related to "cadaver." Creepy. But I
guess words sprout in all directions, and there's
not much you can do about that.

Love,
      Your daughter (alias Rapunzel)

P.S. Do you think I could ask you a few questions about the Evil Spell? I'm thinking about doing a project for school on it. I'm wondering if you ever feel like Rapunzel too.

9:32 a.m.

SATURDAY


Dear #5667,

Mom drove me to the post office. She had it on her calendar: "8:30 a.m. To P.O. w/C."

"You mean you've been writing to this box ever since Dad went into the hospital?" she said as she backed out of our driveway. "What made you do that?"

"I found a letter Dad wrote. It was torn up and stuck down the side of his red chair. I thought that was why the Evil Spell was so bad this time . . . because he had stopped writing to his eudemon."

"Euda . . . what?" Mom turned to look at me, which was not a good idea when you're backing up. Our tires bounced over the curb. We barely missed Mrs. Booth's mailbox post.

"Eudemon," I repeated. "It's a 'good or benevolent spirit.'"

"Hmmm," said my mom.

"Like a fairy godmother," I added.

"I don't understand you and fairy tales," she

said. "I guess that's Dad's imagination you have and not mine. Personally, I like medical thrillers." She ran one hand through her hair, which was approaching the bush stage. She could never be Rapunzel, because her hair grows OUT, not down. "Although, Little Red Riding Hood's not bad. Excellent description of emergency surgery on a high-risk patient."

"Huh?" I said.

"The woodcutter," she said. "When he has to slice open the wolf to get Granny out. I'm glad I don't have to deliver babies with an ax."

She started laughing, which startled me at first because it had been so long since I'd heard her really crack up. She has a great laugh, all fizzy, like soda over lots of ice.

"Dad's getting better, isn't he?" I said.

"Next week," she said. "The doctors think by next week he can come home."

When we got to the post office, I took out the key Dad had told me how to find, and I went into the deserted lobby and opened the glass box. All my letters were packed in there, like chips in a can, one flat against the next. I put them into a plastic bag and took them back to the car.

It's strange seeing my letters again, in one big pile. It's like they aren't from me at all. I have them next to my bed, but I haven't read any of them yet. I think I'm going to wait until I can get under my covers with my flashlight. That way, I can listen.

Later,
    Rapunzel

P.S. There was an article in the paper today about the bridge. The headline was "Landmark To Be Destroyed for Lack of Sponsor." I guess it's going to happen. And there's nothing I can do. I cut out the article for my dad. Even though it'll make him sad, I think he'll want to know.

Dear U.S. Army Corps of Engineers,
New England District,

You don't know me, but I hope you'll listen to me anyway.

There's a bridge that you have to destroy because no one's able to move it and take care of it. You know the one I mean.

I was on that bridge. I shouldn't have been, but I was. It's a long story. But anyway, while I was there, I wrote a few words on one of the pieces of metal near the end of the bridge. You'll see what I mean if you look.

What I'm writing about is this: Since you're going to have to blow up the bridge anyway, do you think I could have that one little piece, the one I wrote on? I don't have any money right now—I used it for the bus fare up there—but I could offer you ten dollars the next time my neighbor pays me for taking care of her plants.

Thank you for helping me (if you can),

Rapunzel

P.S. No, that's not my real name, but please don't hold it against me.

3:13 p.m.

MONDAY

Dear #5667,

Last night, I started to read the letters that I sent to you. (I mean, sent to ME.) But I had to quit after the first one. It was just too much to take, reading it so soon after I just lived it. Maybe I'll save them for a while, maybe even a whole year, and read them on my next birthday.

Except by then I'll have a new pile! One problem is, WOW, do I write A LOT. When I want to, that is. If it's a teacher asking me to do it, it seems different. Like today, Mr. Stanley gave us an assignment to do a book report as if it were a thank-you letter to the author. You know:

*Dear Famous Author,*

*Thank you for introducing me to the culture of the cannibals of Western Evilonia. Before I read your book, I had no idea how to boil an eyeball, and now I know exactly what to do!*

*And your vocabulary! Wow! It's given me great new words to use in everyday conversation, like "spleen" and "cartilage."*

*Not to mention your character development! I got so attached to the main character, Little Joey, with his cute smile and his chubby cheeks, and then—WHAM!—out of the blue, he gets captured by the cannibals in that exciting scene and you don't know what's going to happen next, but you're pretty sure, because they ARE cannibals after all, and then Little Joey just happens to have a radio with him to call for help, and well, need I say it, my heart was POUNDING for several pages!!!!*

*Please write another book EXACTLY LIKE IT!*
*Your devoted fan,*
*Sally Kissyface*

Anyway, I'm sure that's what Mr. Stanley wants. But my brain doesn't work that way. It hears "thank-you letter" and "author" and it goes wild. I start thinking of things I'm NOT thankful for, like how I'd write an anti-thank-you letter to the author of *Jaws* for making me worry about sharks every time I dip a toe in the ocean. (I didn't actually READ *Jaws*, but my mom has a very old copy and I saw the cover and that was enough.) Or I start thinking of the princess in "The Princess and the Pea" and how she might write a thank-you letter to the mattress manufacturer, thanking them for the lousy mattresses that helped her feel that hard little pea and win her prince's heart. Or I go off on this whole idea that an author should thank YOU for reading her book, and not the other way around, and what kinds of things would she thank you for noticing in her work, and what if you did the book report that way????

You see my problem here. The only thing is, I promised my mom I'd at least TRY to do my assignments the way my teachers want them, and so I guess I'll have to send my crazy ideas to you, and pretend to be as normal as possible Monday through Thursday. Not Friday, though. They let me be a little weird on Friday. You wouldn't believe how much that helps.

Got to go do my homework,
    Rapunzel

P.S. I think I'll do my independent study on Evil Spells. There's so much I don't know. Like why they happen. Or who gets zapped. Or when. I guess the doctors might not know either. But somebody has to ask the questions.

P.P.S. I thought of what to say to Andrew. Since we have to be in the GT program together.

Dear Andrew,

A wise Chinese fortune cookie once said, "After a while, even the dog makes a compromise with the cat."

What I'm proposing is this: Don't call me Sugar Buns, don't ask me about my grades, and don't laugh at my poems. Then I promise not to hit you with my English book.

Is it a deal?

Signed,
    The Cat

P.S. I'm not calling you a dog. That's just what the cookie said.

P.P.S. And thanks for telling me about my dad. Nobody else would.

Dear #5667,

Dad came home today. We ordered Chinese food to celebrate and I ate three egg rolls. My dad ate four. And we laughed at our stupid fortunes. Mine said, "You should be able to undertake anything." I guess that means I'm going to be a mortician. Get it? Undertake, undertaker???

My dad's said, "Peace and justice are the jewels of life." I kind of like that. And my mom's was, "Don't peel an egg that isn't cooked." She said it was the first time she ever got cooking advice she could use.

I wonder how the world would be different if our fortunes were as easy to read as those in cookies. How come characters in fairy tales are always getting prophecies or curses or other things told to them about their futures and not us?

I asked Dad that, and he said, "In the real world, you can only understand your life backward."

I said, "But you have to live it forward."

And he said, "Yes, as best you can."

I wanted to write that down. Just in case I have to write fortune cookie messages one day.

Cheers,

    Rapunzel

P.S. This is my last letter to you. My dad gets you back now. But it doesn't matter, because I got a cool present from him for my birthday!

*Dear Cadence,*

*I'm sorry I missed your thirteenth birthday. I don't have a poem as a present to give you, but I hope you'll like this instead.*

*I'm opening a post-office box in your name—#10223. You may use it however you like, as long as you promise me you'll always listen to your own heart.*

*Yours truly,*
*Dad*

Dear #10223,

It's weird calling you by a new name because you're the same person. Like when somebody has always been Fred and suddenly they want you to call them by their middle name, which happens to be Canfield, and you can't ever seem to remember what it is, except that it starts with a "C" and has to do with eating or growing things, which could be "Cauliflower" or "Cotton" or any number of "C" words, except the one you want to remember but can't. This happens to me on tests. I can remember all kinds of things about an important person's name, like the way it sounds like a bad cough followed by a little wheezing, or how the shape of the first name matches the shape of the last name, but I can't think of one letter to write down!

But anyway, the point is: You're mine! And Dad said I could come down to the post office to get my letters whenever he went to get his. Mom thinks we are both a little weird.

"What's wrong with getting her a diary?" she asked Dad.

"Be glad she doesn't want a car," he said, and smiled at me.

"Not yet, anyway." I made sure to point out.

Yours truly,
Your new friend

P.S. I'm going to try to write you every day. Except now I can do it from my kitchen counter, while eating popcorn and drinking root beer. No more Homework Club!!!

3:22 p.m.

THURSDAY

Dear #10223,

Guess what? I heard from the bridge people! They couldn't actually give me a piece of the bridge because of how it's welded together. But they sent me a picture of the whole bridge itself, and thanked me for caring about it. And they said that they were extending the deadline to find a sponsor! After the newspaper article, so many people had written to them about saving the bridge that they're going to try to set up a foundation to rescue it.

I'm going to save the letter and show it to my dad when I'm ready to tell him the whole story.

More later,
   Your secret admirer (ha, ha!)

P.S. I wonder if my dad could use that picture on the cover of his book if he ever gets it published. He isn't writing poems again yet.

11:46 p.m.

FRIDAY

Dear #10223,

Guess what Andrew did today?

We had to say what we had picked for our independent study projects, and I said I'd be researching "Depression: An Evil Spell."

Then, a kid (who will NOT be influential in the next millennium) raised his hand and said, "That doesn't sound scientific to me."

And Andrew, he said, "Hey, she knows what she's doing."

Then that same jerk, he said, "Oooh, looks like Rapunzel has got herself a prince."

Everybody laughed except Andrew and me.

But I didn't let it ruin my day. That kid doesn't know about you, how you're working on me to be a better human being. He doesn't know that I've rescued myself at least once. Most of all, he doesn't know who I really am.

He still thinks I'm Rapunzel.

Your friend,

Cadence Rae Brogan

P.S. I finished that story tonight. Here's the ending:

## THE TRUE STORY OF RAPUNZEL
### (THE CONCLUSION, AS TOLD BY HERSELF)

Could it be the Prince of Happy Endings?

Sure enough, when she looked down at the woods below, there was a young man with a sack over his shoulder. He had dark curly hair that stood out in all directions and muddy black boots. His clothes were plain, and she could see neither sword nor crown, but perhaps this was just a disguise he had taken to pass unnoticed among his people.

"Quick!" she cried. "Toss me up a Happy Ending! There's no time to waste!"

But the young man laughed. "Happy Endings? Who do you think I am? A prince? I'm a poor farmer boy—there's nothing in my sack but apples! But if you wish, I'll toss one up to you, as they're most delicious and I don't mind sharing."

He took a large apple out of his sack and threw it up into the air. But unfortunately for Rapunzel, who would've liked more than watery gruel to eat, the young man did not

182

have a strong throwing arm. Or good aim. No matter how hard he tried, he couldn't throw the apple up high enough or true enough to reach Rapunzel's window. After several tries, the apple was a sorry, bruised version of its formerly delicious self.

"Never mind," called down Rapunzel. "Save your strength. It's no use. I'm going to be locked in here for life anyway. What good will one apple do?"

"Locked up for life?" replied the young man, who had a kind heart. "Well, then. Here's one thing I can do for you. I'll plant this bruised fruit in the ground so that one day its seeds will sprout a tree for you. After many years, it will grow tall enough that you'll be able to pick an apple from its branches."

"Yes!" cried Rapunzel. "That's it!"

And she sat down at her typewriter and pounded out the perfect Happy Ending. (As you may guess, it had to do with the daughter saving her father's heart by planting his apple in the Royal Orchard, but it's not for me or you to know for sure.)

Then Rapunzel wrote a letter to the disgruntled customer:

*Dear Most Unhappy Customer,*

*There IS a Happy Ending to the story you sent me. In fact, I've written it.*
*As for you and YOUR Happy Ending—well—in order to lift the curse, you'll have to write that for yourself, because my typewriter no longer has all of its keys.*

*Good luck,*
　　*Rapun el*

*P.S. Don't worry if your Happy Ending takes a while to sort itself out. I'm still working on mine.*

## THE END